THE LEGEND OF THE IRISH CASTLE

created by
GERTRUDE CHANDLER WARNER

Illustrated by Anthony VanArsdale

Albert Whitman & Company
Chicago, Illinois

Library of Congress Cataloging-in-Publication
data is on file with the publisher.

Copyright © 2016 by Albert Whitman & Company
Published in 2016 by Albert Whitman & Company

ISBN 978-0-8075-0705-6 (hardcover)
ISBN 978-0-8075-0706-3 (paperback)

Printed in the United States of America
10 9 8 7 6 5 4 3 2 LB 20 19 18 17 16

Illustrated by Anthony VanArsdale
Illustrations on pages 95, 96, 98, 99 © Shutterstock.com

For more information about Albert Whitman & Company,
visit our web site at www.albertwhitman.com.

Contents

THE LEGEND OF
THE IRISH CASTLE

CHAPTER 1

The Bad Omen

Henry Alden pushed a cart full of luggage through the bustling airport of Dublin, Ireland. All around him, people were walking very fast and pulling large suitcases. A pilot and two flight attendants wearing navy blue uniforms passed by, their shoes clicking on the tile floor. On the public address system, a voice said, "Last call for flight two-seventeen!" Airports always made the Alden children feel very excited. They loved traveling to new places.

"I wonder how long it will take to get to the castle," said twelve-year-old Jessie Alden. She looked at her watch and reset it to the local time, six hours later than in their home in Greenfield. Between the time change and the long flight, the children were feeling tired. But they had been looking forward to their vacation in Ireland for a long time and couldn't wait to explore the castles and the beautiful countryside.

Grandfather glanced at the map in his hand. "According to the map, it should take about two hours to get to where we're staying."

Grandfather was also carrying Benny, who at six was the youngest Alden. Benny had been asleep when the plane landed and was just starting to wake up. His head rested on Grandfather's shoulder. "Erin, the owner of the castle, said she would pick us up right outside the airport."

Ten-year-old Violet walked ahead of the other children and snapped a picture of a sign that read "This Way to Dublin" with an arrow pointing toward the doors. Violet was planning to make a scrapbook of this adventure when the Aldens returned home, and she thought a picture of the sign would be perfect for the cover.

The automatic doors opened with a *whoosh*, and the Aldens walked out into the sunshine. Taxis were lined up along the curb.

"What a beautiful day!" Violet said, snapping another picture.

"We're lucky the sun is out," Henry said. "I've read that it rains a lot in Ireland."

"We don't mind a little rain," said Violet. She took off her purple sweater and tied it around her waist. "We always found fun things to do on rainy days when we lived in the boxcar!"

After their parents died, the Alden children had run away. They were afraid of their grandfather because they thought he was mean and they wouldn't like living with him. In the woods, the children had found an abandoned boxcar and made it their home. They had lots of adventures, and even found their dog, Watch, in the woods. He became part of their family too. When their grandfather found them, they realized he wasn't mean at all.

Grandfather Alden took the children to his home to live with him and his housekeeper, Mrs. McGregor. Grandfather brought the boxcar to his home, and put it in the backyard to use as a clubhouse.

"That must be our ride," Jessie said, pointing to a white van that said "Duncarraig Castle" in green letters on the side.

Grandfather and the children walked toward the van just as a woman got out. She had a long red braid that hung down over her shoulder. "Céad míle fáilte!" she said. "That means 'a hundred thousand welcomes.' I'm Erin."

The children introduced themselves, and Henry and Erin loaded the luggage into the van. Grandfather helped Benny get buckled in. Benny tried to wake himself up, but as soon as they started driving, he closed his eyes again.

"Poor Benny," said Violet. "He seems so tired."

"You all must be tired after that long trip," Erin said. "And hungry too. Let's stop for lunch when we get to Howth."

Benny sat up and opened his eyes. "Did someone say 'lunch'?"

Everyone laughed. "I thought lunch might wake you up," Grandfather said.

Erin took the scenic route toward the seaside village of Howth. The tall cliffs alongside the road were bright green and towered over the ocean below. White seagulls sailed through the air hunting for fish. Erin told the children about the sights. "Down there is Dublin Bay," she said, pointing to the water. "And that's Baily Lighthouse."

She pointed to a narrow white building perched on the edge of a cliff. It was a steep drop down to the ocean, where the waves crashed against the rocks.

Erin continued. "The village of Howth has been a busy fishing port for hundreds of years, but the fog can make it dangerous. The lighthouse shines to warn the boats when they are getting too close to these cliffs."

Violet shivered thinking about how scary a shipwreck would be. "I'm so glad we traveled by plane instead of boat!" she said.

"I think a ship would be exciting!" Henry said. He was fourteen and liked adventure. "As long as the captain knew what he was doing."

"Don't worry, Violet," Grandfather said. "Ships don't rely on lighthouses anymore. Now they use computers to navigate the ocean, so sailors always know when they are close to land."

Erin parked the van in front of a row of very old buildings painted bright colors. "Let's have lunch on the pier. How do you feel about fish and chips?" she asked Benny.

Grandfather explained, "In Ireland, chips are what we think of as french fries back in the U.S. Fish and chips is a dish of fried fish with fried potatoes on the side."

Benny rubbed his stomach. "I don't mind if they call them fries or chips, as long as they come with ketchup!"

The Aldens sat down at a table covered in a red-checkered cloth, and Erin ordered their food. From where they sat they could watch the boats coming in and out of port. Some raised big nets full of fish onto the pier.

While the Aldens and Erin waited for their food, Jessie pulled out the book she had been reading on the plane.

"That's a good one!" Erin said, looking

at the cover. The book was called *Irish Fairy Legends*. "Maeve Rowe McCarron is very famous. She writes about Irish culture and history. I loved her books when I was younger."

"Until I read this book, I never knew there were so many kinds of fairy creatures in Irish folklore," Jessie said.

"We knew about leprechauns," Violet pointed out. "They're the ones who wear green and hide a pot of gold at the end of a rainbow."

"Mhm," Jessie said. "But we had never heard about the goblin that disguises itself as a chained black horse—the one called a pooka."

"And the creature called a merrow," Henry added. "It lives in the sea like a mermaid, but instead of a fish tail, it wears seal skins."

Grandfather noticed that both Benny and Violet were looking nervous. They weren't sure whether they wanted to meet creatures like these on their trip. "But remember," Grandfather said, "these creatures are part of myths. Myths are stories, but not everything in them is real."

"Just like ghosts," Henry said. "We know

from solving mysteries that when we think we see a ghost, there's always another explanation."

Just then, the waitress brought their food. All the children had ordered fish and chips, which came in wicker baskets lined with waxed paper. Grandfather and Erin had ordered mussels, and those came in bowls full of broth. They also had brown bread and fresh butter. The food smelled delicious.

"I don't know," Erin said, as she used a fork to pull a mussel from its black shell, "in Ireland, lots of people believe in banshees."

Jessie took a bite of fish and flipped a few pages in her book to the paragraph she was looking for. *"A banshee is a female spirit,"* she read aloud. *"Her cry can sound like a woman wailing or an owl moaning. She is often depicted wearing a gray hooded cloak. The presence of a banshee is known to be a bad omen."*

"What's a bad omen?" asked Benny. "It sounds…*bad*."

"I think it means bad luck," Henry said.

"Some of the old Irish families had their very own banshees," Erin said. "Like the family that once owned Duncarraig Castle.

Their banshee warned them when something bad was about to happen."

"Do you think *we* will see the banshee?" Benny asked.

Erin laughed. "Let's hope not!"

But Violet couldn't help noticing that Erin's fork was trembling when she took a bite. Talking about the banshee seemed to make her awfully uneasy.

CHAPTER 2

A Sound of Wailing

After lunch, the Aldens piled back into the van and Erin drove along the coastal road and through the countryside for more than an hour. They passed through a few small villages with fenced cottages and churches covered in ivy, and the van bumped over the cobblestones of the old roads. Finally, Erin turned down a long, narrow lane that led through the trees. The sun had gone behind the clouds and it was starting to sprinkle.

"Now *this* is the Irish weather I was

expecting," Henry said. "But maybe after the rain we'll see a rainbow."

"I'd sure like to get a picture of one for the scrapbook!" Violet said.

They came into a clearing, and up ahead was an enormous gray stone castle. Fuzzy green moss was growing on some of the stones. Off to the side was a garden full of climbing vines and lush flowers, with a bench where you could sit and admire the view. Behind the castle was a soft meadow of yellow and green grass, and a deep woods with a single path cutting through.

"Welcome to Duncarraig Castle!" Erin said. "The most beautiful castle in Ireland!"

The children got out of the van and stretched their legs.

"That's funny," Benny said, looking around. "I don't see any dunes around here."

"Duncarraig is an Irish word," Erin said. "*Dun* means fort, and *carraig* means a rocky headland, like the rocks along the coast. Castles were usually named for their locations, so Duncarraig means the fort by the rocky headlands."

"We could call the boxcar Fortfence,"

Benny said. "Because it is kind of like our fort, and it's near the fence in the backyard."

Henry laughed. "That's true, Benny. Now, let's carry in the bags," he said.

Jessie zipped the book about fairy legends back into her bag and joined Henry. "I'll help you."

Violet took Benny's hand, and Grandfather followed as they walked up the path, gravel crunching under their feet. Erin opened the heavy wooden door of the castle by pulling on the iron ring. It looked very old and creaked on its hinges.

The children entered the dark front hall, where woven tapestries hung on the walls. A long wooden table held flickering candles.

"We've spent the last few years fixing up this place," Erin told them. "It seems like a fun idea to stay in a hotel in an old castle, until you realize that people who lived in castles didn't have plumbing or electricity! So we made the rest of the rooms modern for the hotel guests. But we decided to leave the front hall just as it had been for hundreds of years. A little piece of history."

Violet pointed her camera at the iron chandelier hanging far above them from the high ceiling and took a picture. "Just think how many people have walked through this hall in all that time!" she said.

"And how tall the ladder must be for changing the light bulbs!" Grandfather said.

This made Erin laugh. "That's my Uncle Fergus's job," she said. "You'll meet him soon." She pointed to the carved wooden staircase. "Your room is this way."

Benny and Violet rushed up the stairs and everyone else followed. They walked down a long hallway on the second floor. On one side was a dark wood balcony that looked down over the main hall downstairs. On the other side were windows so deep, you could sit inside the windowsill.

Benny climbed up into one and looked out at the woods behind the castle. "I don't see any banshees," he said.

As they walked, Erin pointed to a room with an open door. Inside was a small sofa and a desk overflowing with paper. A butterfly made of different colored glass hung in the window and when the sun shone through, it cast the colors on the floor. "That's my room. Feel free to knock on my door any time."

They walked on. Henry and Jessie moved more slowly than the others, since they were carrying the luggage. Jessie glanced into a few of the guest rooms they passed. The beds were neatly made with colorful quilts, and many of the rooms had fireplaces.

"All these rooms are empty, Henry," Jessie said. "I expected more guests."

"Me too," Henry said. "It must have cost Erin a lot of money to fix up this old castle. I hope she is booking enough rooms to keep it in business!"

One door on the right was closed. "Looks like someone's staying in that room," Jessie said. "At least that's something."

At the end of the hallway, Erin led them into a large double room joined by a bathroom in the middle. They decided Grandfather would take the big bed on one side, and the children would share the two beds on the other side. Erin said she would give them time to get settled, and left to go back downstairs.

The Aldens went into their room and started to unpack their suitcases. Benny took out a pair of shoes and put them on the table while he sorted his pants and shirts into two piles, and then put them inside the dresser drawer. When he looked up, a tall man with a gray beard and a blue denim work shirt was standing right next to him. The man was frowning.

Benny jumped, surprised, but he didn't want to be rude. "Oh, hello," Benny said nervously. "Are you a guest at the castle too?"

"Name's Fergus," the man said in a gruff voice. "I'm the caretaker."

Jessie stepped forward and offered her hand. "It's nice to meet you, sir. Erin said that you're her uncle. We're the Aldens, visiting from America."

Fergus shook her hand, but he didn't smile. He stared at Benny's shoes, and Violet quickly moved them off the table and onto the floor.

"I was coming in to fix the latch on the window," he said. "The last guest told us it was stuck." He went over to the window and examined the old iron latch for a moment. He tried twisting it, then sprayed some oil around the metal. It squeaked, but after a few more tries, he got the latch to twist and was able to open the window.

"Well, now that's done," Fergus said. He brushed impatiently past the children on his way out of the room, but he stopped when he saw the contents of Jessie's bag lying on one of the beds. On top was the book by Maeve

Rowe McCarron that she had been reading at lunch. Fergus looked at the book and his eyebrows went up. Then he stormed off into the hallway.

"I know one reason why Erin's having trouble getting guests for the hotel," Henry said. "Fergus is not very friendly."

After the children finished unpacking, they went downstairs. Erin was at the front desk with a calculator and a stack of papers. Her forehead was creased, but when she saw the Aldens coming, she broke into a smile. Jessie told her that they had met Fergus upstairs.

"I'm sorry if my uncle seemed grumpy," Erin said, setting down her pen. "He has always lived in the caretaker's cottage out in the woods, but he just recently moved into the castle. It's taking him a little time to get used to being around the people who work here in the hotel now—this year we hired a new kitchen helper and a full-time chef."

"That does seem like it would be a hard change," Violet said, thinking about the days when the children first moved in with their grandfather. The Aldens had had a very different childhood from other children they knew, and it took time for them to adjust too. Plus, Violet liked to try to see the best in people. "He seems like he's very good at his job. It only took him a minute to fix our window."

"That's true," said Henry. "Maybe if I offer to help him with his work, it will cheer him up."

"That's the spirit!" Erin said. "Fergus knows this place inside and out."

Just then, Benny yawned. "Could we start helping tomorrow?" he asked Jessie. "I am feeling a little sleepy."

"Of course!" Erin said. "You all must have jet lag! Even though it's early evening here, your body is still on Boston time and thinks it's time for bed. Best to get some rest."

The Aldens went back upstairs to their room and changed into pajamas. Violet went in to tell Grandfather that they were turning in, but he had already fallen asleep with his book on his chest. The children got under the quilts and even though the sun was still shining, they fell asleep.

Several hours later, Jessie heard Benny say, "What's that noise?"

She opened her eyes. It was very dark in the room, and the digital clock on the nightstand said it was two in the morning. Violet sat up next to her. Henry was still asleep in the other bed next to Benny.

"What noise?" Jessie asked.

"I heard a…wailing sound," Benny whispered.

"I heard it too," Violet said, sounding concerned.

Jessie got out of bed and went to the window. Just as she had guessed, it was still open from when Fergus had fixed the latch. "It's just the wind, blowing through this open window." She pushed it closed and twisted the latch, and the wailing sound stopped.

Benny and Violet joined Jessie at the window. "See," Jessie said. "Nothing to be afraid of. I know it's hard, but we should try to go back to sleep until morning so we can get over this jet lag."

But Benny was still looking out the window. "Look!" he said, pointing to the dark meadow behind the castle. Far away near the edge of the woods, a mysterious figure was moving through the grass, hunched over and carrying a lantern.

"Is that a woman?" Violet asked.

"I can't tell," Benny said. "She has a hood pulled up on her head."

"A hood!" Jessie said, remembering her book on fairy legends. Just then, even though the window was tightly closed, the Aldens heard the wailing sound again. There was only one Irish fairy creature that appeared as a woman with a hood, and made a wailing sound—a banshee!

CHAPTER 3

New Guests

In the morning, the Aldens felt groggy after their night of interrupted sleep. Jessie had finally convinced Benny and Violet that they were safe in their room from whoever had been out in the meadow, and the children went back to sleep. As they all entered the dining room for breakfast, Jessie filled Henry in on what they had seen while he was sleeping.

"And you couldn't see a face?" Henry whispered as they sat down in the high-back chairs.

"No," Jessie said. "But it was definitely someone older because of the way the person walked." She hunched her shoulders forward to demonstrate.

Henry nodded. "Well, we know one thing for sure—it can't be a banshee because they aren't real."

"Actually," Violet whispered, "we don't know that for *sure*. Erin seems to believe in banshees, and she said a lot of other people in Ireland do too." She nudged Benny and pointed to the napkin beside his plate. The children all placed their napkins in their laps.

Jessie shook her head. "I still think there has to be another explanation. Remember how we saw one door closed upstairs yesterday? There are other guests here. Maybe one of them was out taking a walk last night."

Just then, a couple the Aldens hadn't seen before came into the dining room. The man was wearing a gray jacket and had a neatly trimmed beard. The woman had on a frilly yellow dress and a scarf tied in her hair.

"Well, look, dear!" the woman said, clasping her hands at her chest. "There are children here! Aren't they just adorable!"

Jessie didn't like it when adults talked this way, but she smiled politely. "Good morning," she said. "My name's Jessie."

"Mrs. Arthur Davison," she said, holding out her hand and wiggling her fingers to show off a sparkling diamond ring. "We just got married last week!"

"Congratulations!" Violet said. "You must be on your honeymoon."

"Pleased to meet you, kids," her husband said. "And, yes, we are. We plan to travel all over Ireland this week. In fact, we're checking out of the castle this morning to head off to Galway."

"Some honeymoon," Mrs. Davison said with a pout. "I had no idea an old castle would be so boring. There is absolutely *nothing* going on here, and nothing to do but watch the birds. We should have gone to London instead."

Mr. Davison smiled. Violet noticed that he seemed like a pretty patient man, unlike his wife. How could anyone think there was nothing to do in such an interesting place? "Mrs. Davison likes restaurants and concerts, but I for one *like* bird-watching," he said with a wink.

Mr. and Mrs. Davison were both very tall and slim, and stood up straight. Jessie realized that probably meant neither of them could be the mysterious figure. Still, she thought it couldn't hurt to ask whether they had been in the meadow yesterday. "Have you spotted any interesting birds late at night?" Jessie asked.

Henry realized why Jessie was asking, and added, "You'd probably need a lantern if you were out there in the dark."

Mr. Davison gave Henry and Jessie a funny look. "It's best to bird-watch during the day. Owls are the only nocturnal bird around here. And though I do usually take evening walks back at home, so far I've stuck to early mornings on this visit."

"We've been reading our novels and going to bed early every night. It has been quite dull!" Mrs. Davison said.

The figure the Aldens had seen couldn't have been one of the Davisons, Jessie knew. But maybe they could give the children some clues to use in their investigation. "Did you happen to notice anything strange out your window around two in the morning?" Jessie asked.

"If only!" Mrs. Davison said. Suddenly, she looked intrigued. "Why—did *you* see anything strange? That sounds exciting!"

"Just a person taking a walk," Jessie said carefully. If Mrs. Davison was the kind of person who treated children like babies, she probably wouldn't take their investigation very seriously either.

Fergus came into the dining room then and poured himself a cup of coffee from the silver urn sitting on the buffet table. He sat down a few chairs away from Henry and nodded to the guests.

"Good morning, Fergus," Benny said, sitting up a little straighter and folding his hands in his lap. He still felt bad about putting his shoes on the table up in the guest room the day before. He wanted to make sure Fergus knew that the Alden children usually had very nice manners.

"Morning," Fergus said. "Tell me—what have you children learned about Ireland so far?"

Jessie was glad to see that Fergus was in a brighter mood. "Well," she said. "We learned about the lighthouse at Howth."

"And fish and chips!" Benny said.

Fergus laughed. His face looked very different and much kinder when he smiled, but it was a rare occurrence. "Well, if you behave yourselves, I'll play my fiddle for you sometime. Then you can hear some authentic Irish music too."

"We'd like that!" Henry said.

"Fergus," Violet said. "We were just talking with Mr. and Mrs. Davison about someone we saw walking out in the meadow in the middle of the night. Do you know of anyone around here who does that?"

Fergus tightened his jaw and stood up, his mood totally changed. "There's no one else living around this land. You won't find anyone if you go looking—so don't bother trying!" He stormed out, leaving his half-full coffee cup sitting on the table.

"I thought he was happier today, but now he seems angry again," Benny said. "He doesn't like it when we ask questions."

Henry nodded. "Remember, Erin told us that he is having a hard time adjusting. Maybe he's just having a bad day."

The Davisons went over to the table to refill their coffees on the other side of the room. "Well," Jessie whispered so they couldn't hear. "If it wasn't the other guests, and there isn't anyone else staying in the hotel or living around the property, maybe it was Erin we saw out walking."

"She doesn't really slouch, though," Violet said quietly.

"That's true," Jessie said. "If it *was* her, she may not like it that we noticed, and if it *wasn't* her, she may be worried about who it could be. Either way, it's probably best if we don't say anything."

"I agree," Henry said. "Let's look out again tonight—I'll stay awake this time too. Maybe we'll see the figure again."

Grandfather joined them in the dining room just as Erin came in carrying a large tray of food. Her foot caught on the edge of the rug and she started to lose her balance. Grandfather helped steady her, and Henry rushed over to take the tray. He brought it over to the table and Erin passed the plates around. The Davisons sat back down in their chairs with their steaming cups of coffee.

"Well, that was bad luck!" Grandfather said.

"Or good luck," Henry said, "since you *almost* fell, but didn't."

Erin took a deep breath. She seemed a little shaken up, especially when she heard the word "luck." Soon, though, she regained her composure and gestured to the food. "This is a what we call a 'full breakfast' in Ireland," Erin said. "Eggs, rashers—that's what we call bacon—toast, black pudding, and a fried tomato. I hope you like it!"

"It smells delicious," Grandfather said, digging in.

"What's black pudding?" Benny asked, poking it with his fork. "Does it have chocolate in it?"

Erin smiled. "No, it's not a dessert. It's kind of like sausage. But traditional Irish pudding is made with pigs' blood. That's what turns it black."

The children's eyes went wide. Jessie tried hard to keep her manners. "Well. That sounds…very interesting."

Erin laughed. "It's okay if you don't want to eat that part."

The guests ate their breakfasts, and Erin bustled around the table pouring orange juice. "How did everyone sleep?" she asked.

"Pretty well," Benny said. "Except for when we saw the banshee. I wonder if we'll see it again tonight."

"Benny!" Jessie said. She sometimes forgot that Benny was still pretty little, and blurted things out when he shouldn't. She hadn't wanted to worry Erin with talk of a banshee.

"Oops," Benny said.

"Banshee?" Erin asked. Her face went pale and she sank down into an empty chair, holding the pitcher of orange juice in her lap.

Mrs. Davison perked up. "Oh, I knew these little ones were keeping a secret!" She turned to her husband. "This changes everything, darling. We have to see if the castle is really haunted. Let's stay another night."

Erin perked up. "Well, we'd be glad to have you!" she said.

Jessie nodded at Henry, remembering how they'd wondered whether the hotel was getting enough business.

"Except," Erin said, frowning, "your room is already booked for tonight, by some new guests arriving today. The only double-occupancy room we have left is the other large suite. But it's quite a bit more expensive."

Mrs. Davison clutched her husband's arm. "Well, it *is* a special occasion," she said to him.

Mr. Davison smiled. "That's true. We only have one honeymoon. We'll take it!"

"Wonderful," Erin said. "I'll go get it straightened up for you right away." She set down the pitcher on the buffet table and hurried out of the dining room. The Davisons left to gather their things as well.

As the Aldens finished their breakfast, Violet noticed that once again it had started to rain. "I guess we won't be going outside this morning," she said.

"Well, there's lots more of the castle to explore," said Henry.

"Good idea," Jessie said. She cleared the dishes from their places and put them back on the tray, and the children went out into the hallway. They walked in the opposite direction of the staircase, to another wing of the castle that held the kitchen. Past that, they entered a narrow hallway that led to a dimly lit room. Inside they saw that all four walls were lined with shelves that went all the way up to the ceiling. In the center of the room were two leather sofas and a low table between them.

"A library!" Violet said. "This is the perfect place to spend a rainy morning."

A tall ladder with wheels that ran on a track halfway up made it possible to reach books on the highest shelf anywhere in the room. Benny couldn't resist climbing up it.

"Careful, Benny," Henry said. "That ladder looks pretty old." He went over to help his brother down and noticed a large photo on the desk by the window.

"Hey," Henry said, "look at this."

The picture showed a black-and-white image of a young man wearing a fisherman's sweater.

"I wonder how old this picture is," Jessie said. "Something about that man looks very familiar."

"Yes, it does," said Violet, squinting at it. Then she said, "I know—he looks like Erin!"

Benny picked up the frame and walked toward the door. "Maybe we could ask Erin who this is."

"She wouldn't keep his picture on display if he was a secret," Violet pointed out.

Just as Benny was about to go into the hallway, he noticed Fergus down at the end opening a cupboard door. He didn't know anyone was watching him. After a quick glance over his shoulder, Fergus took something out of a box and slipped it into his pocket.

Then Fergus closed the cupboard and walked toward the library. Benny scurried back in, eager to stay out of Fergus's way.

But Henry was convinced that Fergus was just having a bad day, and he tried again to be friendly. "Good morning again," Henry called with a smile, and Fergus stepped into the library.

"Reading, eh?" Fergus said grumpily.

"Yes, and wondering about the history of this place," Henry said. He held up the picture frame. "Do you know if this is a picture of Erin's father?"

Fergus set his mouth into a line and stared at them. "It's best if you don't ask," he said. "You kids need to find something to do, and stop asking so many questions!" He left the room.

The children looked at each other with wide eyes. "It definitely seems like Fergus is hiding something," Jessie said.

"Fergus *is* hiding something," Benny said. "In his pocket." He described how he had seen Fergus take something out of the hallway cupboard.

Henry nodded. "Something strange is happening around here."

Chapter 4

An Unwelcome Gift

By afternoon the rain had finally stopped, and Grandfather found the children sitting in the library looking through old books. Violet had found a botanical guide full of drawings of the different kinds of flowers that could be found growing in this part of Ireland. Jessie was curled up in a chair by the window with *Irish Fairy Legends*. She had almost finished it.

"Down the road a little way is an old manor house that has a traditional walled garden,"

Grandfather said. "Would you like to come with me to see it?"

Benny was the first to leap up and put his book on the shelf. He was restless after being stuck inside all morning, and ready to get outside for some fresh air. "Let's go!" he said.

The children changed into boots Erin called "Wellies" that she kept on hand for guests in a variety of sizes. They were bright yellow with handles on the sides, and would keep the children from getting too muddy as they tromped around in the fields. Violet brought her camera along, and Grandfather took an umbrella just in case.

They walked about half a mile down the winding lane to the manor house. Beside it were tall stone walls that looked like they'd been standing for hundreds of years. You couldn't see what was beyond them. The caretaker of the property let the Aldens in through a door in the wall using an old skeleton key. The children gasped at what was inside—the most beautiful garden they'd ever seen!

A narrow stone path curved through fruit trees and lavender and thorny roses. Off in one corner were peony bushes taller than Benny, in pink and white. Birds hopped from branch to branch.

Violet sat down on a stone bench beside a fountain in the shape of a fish that spit water into a mossy pond. She snapped pictures of the big goldfish swimming in circles in the water.

"Look, Violet," Benny said, "violets!" He pointed at a large planter full of purple flowers.

Violet smiled. "This is my favorite place in Ireland so far," she said.

"Are the walls to keep people out?" Jessie asked Grandfather.

"Or maybe animals that would eat the plants?" Henry wondered.

"Actually, the walls keep the plants warmer, and protect them from the wind," Grandfather said. He pointed to an opening in one of the walls that was charred black around the edges. "This wall is hollow," he said, "so the gardener can build a fire inside it and warm up the garden. That way, he can grow grapes and peaches and other things that normally wouldn't survive in this colder climate."

"Peaches?" Benny asked, his eyes wide.

"Well, it's too early in the season for them to be ripe, I'm afraid," Grandfather said. "But the trees are very beautiful!"

The children explored the garden for a while longer, until Jessie noticed it was getting late and they decided to walk home. As they came up the road toward the castle near dusk, Benny noticed a lilac bush growing along the fence at the edge of the castle's property.

"Look, Violet," he said, "more purple flowers!"

Grandfather told the children he was going inside to read the newspaper. "Being out of the country is no excuse to skip the crossword puzzle," he said cheerfully.

The children said they'd see him inside, and lingered by the fence. Jessie knelt down and smelled the lilacs.

"Wow, these smell so pretty," Jessie said.

"Let's take some inside to Erin," suggested Benny. "She can put them in a vase of water on the front desk."

"Yes, great idea," Henry said as he broke off a branch. Benny carried the lilacs proudly up the lane to the door of the castle.

But just as they were about to go inside, Fergus appeared and put his arm across the door.

"What are you trying to do? You can't bring those in here!" Fergus barked, looking at the lilacs.

Jessie felt her stomach drop. She realized maybe they had been wrong to pick the flowers without asking permission. "We're sorry, Fergus," she said.

He shook his head and stalked off.

"Uh-oh," Violet said. "I think we made a mistake."

"Let's put the branch back where we found it," said Henry. "And when we get back inside, we'll apologize to Erin too." The other Aldens nodded their agreement.

Back near the fence, they set the branch on the ground beside the lilac bush. Just as they were about to head back inside, Benny froze. "What's that?" he said, sounding afraid.

He pointed to the opposite side of the meadow, where the woods began. It was the same spot they had been able to see from their room on the second floor. The tall hedges along the edge of the property were rustling, as if someone or something was moving them.

"Is someone watching us?" Jessie wondered aloud.

"Maybe it's just the wind," Henry said, glancing around. But none of the other trees were moving as much as that one spot in the hedges.

Benny looked very worried. "What if it's a pooka?" he said.

"It's not," Jessie told him. "Pookas are just myths. And anyway, the pooka is the horse that drags its chains. If that was a pooka, we'd be able to hear the chains."

"But it's not," Henry added, "because pookas aren't real."

"I'm still not sure," Violet said. "A lot of people believe in these creatures, and I might too."

"Let's go look at the book again," Jessie said, "and I'll show you what I mean about the pooka."

The children went inside the castle and

back to the library where they had been reading earlier in the day.

"See, Benny," Jessie said, crossing over to one of the leather couches. "In the book it says—wait." Jessie stopped and looked around. "Where did my book go? I left it right here before we went to the gardens with Grandfather. I'm sure of it." She looked among the books and newspapers stacked on a shelf nearby, but her book wasn't there.

"You don't think someone could have moved it? Maybe Erin was cleaning up." Henry said.

But the rest of the books still lay on the table, right where the children had left them.

Jessie felt a shiver. "I think my book has... disappeared," she said.

"Yikes!" Benny said.

CHAPTER 5

The Familiar Figure

The search for the missing book was interrupted when Grandfather found them in the library and told them it was time for dinner. The children followed him into the dining room and took their places around the large table set with white linen napkins embroidered with *DC* for Duncarraig Castle.

Erin poured water in the goblets on the table. Mr. and Mrs. Davison were already seated, and were chatting with the new guests that had arrived that morning, Robert and George. They told the Aldens they were visiting from Canada, and planned to play as many rounds of golf in Ireland as they could. Both men were dressed in garish plaid pants and brightly colored shirts. George pulled out a lime-green knitted tam with a huge pompon sewed to the top.

"Whoever has the losing score has to wear this," George said, and Erin laughed.

George laughed too. "Half the fun of golf is the ridiculous outfits."

Robert nodded in agreement, then turned to the children. "Mrs. Davison tells us that you kids spotted a banshee out your window the other night," Robert said. He had spiky gray hair and round pink cheeks. "George here doesn't believe in ghosts, but I am inclined to be open-minded. A country with such a long history is bound to be full of spirits."

"Well, we aren't actually sure *what* we saw," Henry said. "I think there must be another explanation."

"Henry, you sound like a very sensible young man," George said. "The only spirit

I'd be willing to believe in is one who can make sure all my putts go in!"

Everyone laughed.

Then Erin said, "Joking aside, we know that all the hotel guests and staff were accounted for that evening. And there isn't anyone else out in this part of the county. So I can't really think of another explanation, *except* for a banshee." She looked at all of her guests. "I think we have to accept that this castle is a little bit haunted."

Jessie gave her siblings a surprised look. Before, Erin had seemed to be half joking when she talked about the castle's banshee, but now she sounded like she actually believed the banshee was real. What had changed?

Mrs. Davison turned to her husband and said, "I am very glad we came to this castle after all, darling. A real banshee!"

Erin and the kitchen helper served the dinner of roast beef and potatoes. After the long day of walking in the fresh air, the children were very hungry and they focused on their food, then helped Erin clear the dishes. After dessert, the adults wanted to linger at the table drinking coffee and tea, and Grandfather told the children they could be excused.

Back in the library, the Aldens sat on the couches to discuss what they had learned about the mysterious figure in the meadow. Jessie was still confused about what Erin had said.

"She seems sure now that the castle is haunted," Jessie said. "Doesn't that seem odd?"

"I was thinking about that," Henry said. "But I think I know why."

"Because the banshee is real?" Benny asked in a frightened voice.

Henry shook his head. He put a comforting hand on Benny's shoulder. "There's no reason to be scared, Benny. Remember, banshees are just part of old stories."

"Then why would Erin say she believes the castle is haunted?" Violet asked.

"This morning, Mr. and Mrs. Davison were about to check out, remember?" Henry said. "But then when they heard about the banshee, Mrs. Davison wanted to stay for another night. Erin is talking about the banshee because a haunted castle is good for business!"

Jessie nodded. "Now, that makes sense."

She thought for a moment and an idea came to her. "Do you think *Erin* is pretending to be the banshee? Dressing up in the hood and walking around at night, wailing?"

Henry snapped his fingers. "That could explain why Fergus doesn't want us exploring the property. If we uncover what she's doing, then the guests will know that the castle isn't haunted after all and they might take their business somewhere else."

"I don't know," Violet said. "Erin seems like such a kind person. I don't think she would lie to us."

"Either way, we have to find out," Jessie said.

"We can watch out the window again tonight," suggested Benny. "And maybe we'll be able to see if the banshee is really Erin."

"But we need a way to be able to see for sure," Jessie said. "Last time, we couldn't see the figure's face because he or she was too far away."

Henry noticed a pair of binoculars guests used for bird-watching sitting on the desk beside the window. "We could borrow these," he said, picking them up. "Maybe then we could get a better look at the figure's face."

The children took the binoculars up to their room and set them on the windowsill, then returned to the library to read. Soon, Grandfather joined them with his newspaper. Erin built a fire in the library fireplace, and the Aldens tried to concentrate on their books. Even though they appeared relaxed on the outside, they were impatient for the evening to pass. They couldn't wait for it to get dark, and for bedtime to come, so they could start watching the meadow behind the castle. They didn't want to raise anyone's suspicions by going to bed early. If Erin was pretending to be the banshee, she might stay home if she thought the children were planning to watch.

Finally all four Alden children had brushed their teeth and put their pajamas on. Sitting on the beds in their room, they made a plan.

"Violet and I will take the first shift," Jessie said, writing down the schedule on a piece of paper in her notebook. "I'll take notes on anything odd we see. At midnight, we'll wake Benny and Henry up to take over while we sleep."

Henry nodded. He went over to the door that opened onto a small balcony on the same side of the room as the window where they'd seen the mysterious figure the night before. "You might be able to get a better look from out here," Henry said.

Henry and Benny got into bed, and the girls stepped out into the night air. On the balcony, they could hear crickets chirping in the tall grass and watched an owl dive from a tree branch to catch a brown mouse.

Violet looked at the side of the castle that was visible from where they stood. Many of the hotel's guest rooms remained unfilled and the windows were dark. But there were a few lights on. Violet noticed that one of the windows lit by a lamp had a butterfly shape hanging on the pane.

She pointed it out to Jessie. "That's Erin's room," Violet said.

Jessie nodded. "That's right—I remember the butterfly sun catcher."

"If her light's on, that probably means she's in her room," Violet said nervously.

Jessie had to agree. "I don't think she would

leave the light on if she was going out," Jessie said. "She probably can't afford to waste electricity with all the other expenses she has running this place."

"And if she's in her room," Violet said, "that means she can't be the one pretending to be a banshee!"

"Well, let's wait and see," Jessie said. "Maybe no one will come out tonight."

The sky grew darker as Jessie and Violet watched and waited. To keep from getting bored, they counted how many stars were in the sky, and tried to name the many types of plants they had seen in the walled garden with Grandfather. The time passed slowly.

Around midnight, Jessie went inside to wake the boys, and Violet stayed outside with the binoculars. She was polishing the lenses with the cuff of her sleeve when she heard a noise in the meadow, a low wailing sound. Violet put the binoculars up to her eyes, her heart pounding. She panned across the meadow, along the tree line, in the direction of the noise. And then she saw it! It was the same figure from the night before, wearing the same gray hood.

"Jessie," Violet called in an urgent whisper. "Hurry!"

Jessie rushed back out onto the balcony and took the binoculars. She looked through the eyepiece and moved the dial on top to focus in on the figure.

Violet's hand flew up to her mouth, and she pointed to the window with the butterfly. "Jessie, Erin's light is still on in her room. Oh, this is all so spooky!"

"That figure I see is definitely not Erin," Jessie said. "And I don't think it's a ghost either. But..."

Just then the boys came out, rubbing their eyes and trying to wake up.

"But what?" Benny asked.

Jessie shook her head and lowered the binoculars in surprise. "I can't explain it, but her face looks so familiar somehow!"

"Familiar?" Henry asked, holding out a hand. "Here, let me have a look."

But just as he raised the binoculars to his eyes, the figure disappeared into the woods once more.

CHAPTER 6

A Creature in the Forest

The Aldens didn't fall asleep until almost one in the morning, so the next day they slept later than usual. Violet woke up first, and roused Jessie and her brothers so they'd have enough time to get dressed and into the dining room before they missed breakfast.

The promise of more eggs and bacon made Benny get ready faster than anyone else. While the others tied their shoes, he looked out the window.

"The meadow is gone," Benny said.

"Gone?" asked Henry.

"And the woods too, and the garden," Benny said. "It's all gone."

Jessie gave Violet a funny look, and they joined Benny at the window. In a way, the youngest Alden was right. From where they stood, they could no longer see anything that was more than a few feet away from the window.

"Benny, I can see why you'd think that, but don't worry. The meadow is still there. We just can't see it because of the fog." Jessie said.

"It's the thickest fog I've ever seen!" Henry said.

Benny remembered their lunch on the pier at Howth when they'd first arrived. "Now I can see why those ships needed the lighthouse," he said. "You can't see *anything* out there."

"We'd better go," Jessie said after checking her watch. "It's nearly ten o'clock." The children hurried down the stairs and into the main hall. Mrs. Davison stood at the front desk, and Grandfather and Mr. Davison were just coming back inside after loading the

Davisons' luggage in their car. Mrs. Davison was wearing a large yellow hat and sunglasses.

"Oh, just look at these little darlings," Mrs. Davison said to her husband. "Could they be any cuter?" Jessie tried not to let the comment bother her. She knew that Mrs. Davison had good intentions, but some people just didn't know how to talk to children.

"Well, kids," Mr. Davison said. "This is good-bye." He shook Grandfather's hand and gave the children high fives. "We're off to Galway this morning."

"In a convertible!" Mrs. Davison said.

"I hope you enjoy the rest of your honeymoon," said Violet. "May I take your picture for my scrapbook?"

The couple posed together. "I hope you find the banshee," Mrs. Davison said as she smiled for the picture. "Make sure to keep us posted!" She wrote down her email address on a slip of paper and gave it to Jessie, who stuck it inside the pages of her notebook.

Erin was behind the desk checking out the Davisons. She gave them a receipt. "Thank you very much for staying at Duncarraig

Castle. Please be careful driving in this terrible fog!"

The Davisons went out to the circle drive in front, where a yellow convertible was parked. It was so bright they had no trouble seeing it in the fog.

"The car matches Mrs. Davison's hat," Benny said.

Jessie laughed. "It sure does!" Grandfather and the children waved to the newlyweds as they drove away.

Henry glanced in Erin's direction and noticed that the bright smile she'd had while saying good-bye had fallen away, and her forehead was once again creased with worry.

"Is everything all right, Erin?" Henry asked.

She looked out the window again and muttered to herself. "I just hope the road between here and Dublin is clear."

"Me too," Henry said. But after he thought for a moment about what she had said, he paused. "Why the road between here and Dublin? Aren't the Davisons heading west to Galway, not toward Dublin?"

"Or maybe you are expecting more new guests today, arriving from Dublin?" Grandfather asked.

"Yes," Erin said, absentmindedly. Then she looked up from the front desk computer. "I mean...no! There are no guests arriving today. Please excuse me." She rushed around from behind the desk, accidentally knocking over a stack of papers. The children rushed over to help pick them up, but she waved them away. "Don't worry," she said. "I'll get them." Erin gathered all the papers in her arms and rushed off down the hallway.

"What was *that* all about?" Jessie whispered to Violet and the boys.

They shook their heads, bewildered. Something was definitely bothering Erin, but they had no idea what it could be.

* * *

Grandfather decided to take a nap after breakfast, so the children set out to explore the castle grounds and see if they could learn any more about the figure Jessie had seen through the binoculars. Now that they were sure it wasn't Erin, they didn't have any other guesses for who it could be.

As the day grew warmer, the fog was starting to lift, but it was still too hard to see very far in the distance. The Aldens walked across the broad meadow and entered the woods on the path that cut between the trees. Inside the forest, it was much darker than out in the field. They walked for a few minutes and came to a fork where the path split in two directions.

"Maybe we should split up," Jessie said.

"I don't know," Benny said. "What if the banshee is down one of these paths?"

"He won't be," Henry said confidently, "but I still don't think we should split up. We don't know these woods at all, and we don't want anyone to get lost."

"I agree," Violet said, taking Benny's hand. "Let's stick together."

The children chose the path that curved to the left because it was wider and looked like it had been used more often than the other path. They walked for a few minutes in the quiet, surrounded by green on all sides. The forest floor was covered with ivy and ferns, and the boughs above them were thick with leaves. Moss grew on the tree trunks, so even they were green.

Just then, they heard a rustling sound off to the side of the path. The Aldens froze, and Benny squeezed Violet's hand. A creature walked out of the bushes and onto the path in front of them. It was gray, with shaggy fur and a long pink tongue.

"Is that a...wolf?" Benny asked in a small voice.

"It's a dog!" Jessie whispered. "A *big* dog."

From farther down the path came a call. "Arooo," the voice said. Violet pulled out her camera and scrambled to turn it on.

The dog responded with its own call. "Awooooo," the dog wailed. It stepped off the path and bounded through the trees in the direction of the call before Violet could snap the photo.

"The wailing we've been hearing from our room—it isn't coming from a banshee," she said. "It's coming from a ghost dog!"

CHAPTER 7

The Inscription

As they walked back to the castle, Jessie tried to convince Violet and Benny that what they had seen couldn't possibly be a ghost dog.

"Violet, we know ghosts aren't real," Jessie said, "so that means that ghost *dogs* aren't real either. Anyway, my book on Irish fairy creatures didn't even mention something like that. If only I could find the book, I could show you!"

It was starting to sprinkle again, and the children ran the rest of the way up the lane.

Inside they took off their jackets and hung them on hooks by the front door.

"Maybe we can find another book in the library that would give us more information on...whatever that thing was!" Henry said.

Jessie took a deep breath as they entered the library once more. The room smelled like old books and furniture polish. "It's hard to feel worried in a room like this," she said. "It's the coziest part of the castle."

"Look," Violet said, pointing at the old stone fireplace, where flames crackled on the logs. "Erin even built a fire."

Henry stepped closer to the fireplace to warm his hands. He thought for a moment, then said, "Isn't it strange? Erin said there were no more guests arriving today, but she built this fire, and this morning I saw her checking her email over and over. It really does seem like she is expecting someone. I wonder why she would want to keep that a secret."

Jessie nodded. She had been wondering that too.

The children fanned out across the library in search of clues. Benny pulled down a book about Irish dog breeds and started leafing through it. "Hey!" he said. "I think I found something!"

He laid the book on the low table between the two couches and pointed to a picture. "Doesn't that look like the ghost dog we saw?"

Jessie peered at the text. "That's not a ghost dog," she said. "It's just a dog, a breed called an Irish wolfhound. See, right here it says they have gray fur and long legs."

Henry pointed to a paragraph farther down the page. "And this says the breed is known for its distinctive howl or wail."

Violet gave a sigh of relief and opened another book. "I like real dogs much better than ghost dogs," she said. "And now that I know it was a real dog, I miss Watch!"

Watch, the stray dog the Aldens had found when they were living in the boxcar, was back home in Massachusetts with Mrs. McGregor. They knew he missed them too, but he also liked having the house to himself, especially because Mrs. McGregor felt sorry for him and gave him extra treats when the children were away.

"I miss Watch too," said Benny. "He would loving running in these fields, and he would love rashers!"

The children laughed as they continued browsing the shelves. Henry pulled another book down from a high shelf. "Here's something interesting," he said. "This one is about Irish superstitions." He flipped to a chapter near the back of the book and read for a moment.

"I think I know why Fergus got so upset at Benny the day we were unpacking," Henry said.

"He didn't like that I put my shoes on the table," Benny said. "He probably thought they were dirty."

"It wasn't the dirt that upset him," Henry said. "Putting shoes on a table top is considered bad luck in Ireland." Henry skimmed the list on the page. "And look here—bringing lilacs inside can also bring bad luck!"

"That explains why he didn't want us to bring Erin the bouquet for the front desk," Benny said. "I thought he was upset that we had picked the flowers."

"What if…" Violet said, thinking. "What if Fergus isn't grouchy so much as *nervous*? If he is superstitious and worried about bad luck, and if he heard Erin talking about the banshee, maybe he is worried something bad is going to happen."

"Do you remember when I saw him slipping something in his pocket in the hallway?" Benny asked. "Maybe it was some kind of charm to ward off bad luck, and he didn't want anyone to see him using it."

"There's definitely more to the story with Fergus," said Jessie. She traced her fingers over the spines of the books on the shelf and noticed a name she recognized. "McCarron!" she said, pulling out the book. "This is the same author as my fairy creatures book that went missing. In fact, it's the same book." She showed it to Violet. The title, *Irish Fairy Creatures*, was printed on the cloth cover in gold letters, but the book looked much older than Jessie's copy, and it didn't have a dust jacket.

Violet opened to the title page. "There's an inscription," she said. *"To my dear friend F., who always makes sure I get my writing done."*

Violet handed the book to Henry, and he and Benny looked too.

"I wonder who *F* is," Benny asked. He handed the book back to Jessie, and she turned it over to look at the back, then inside the back cover.

"Well," Violet said, "if this castle has been in Erin's family for a while, her father would own all these books. And remember—we saw his picture on the desk. Or at least we think that's him in the picture. Maybe *his* name starts with an F."

"Frank? Or...Fred?" Jessie suggested.

"*Fergus* starts with an *F*," Benny said.

"That's true," Henry said. "Do you think it could be Fergus? That would mean he knows this author."

Jessie was still looking inside the back of the book.

"What are you looking for?" Henry asked her.

"I have an idea," Jessie said. "But I can't be sure. First I need to find my own copy of this book!" And then she rushed out of the room.

CHAPTER 8

The Famous Face

The other children followed Jessie out into the hallway. She came to the cupboard at the end of the hall, then turned back to Benny.

"Is this the cupboard where you saw Fergus take something out?" she whispered. She wanted to be sure that no one would overhear them.

Benny nodded, and Jessie opened the door. Inside was a box with a picture of a dog on it.

"Treats!" Benny said. "These are the same kind we have at home for Watch. I never heard of anyone using treats as a good luck charm."

Jessie laughed, and put some of the treats in her pocket. "I think he was using the treats for something else," she said. "Come on. I'll show you."

Jessie and the rest of the Aldens ran to the great hall where they had first entered the castle. Fresh candles were burning on the candlesticks, and there was a plate of warm cookies on the table.

"Another sign that a new guest is coming," Violet said, and the other children agreed.

"Maybe Fergus will know where your book is, Jessie," Henry suggested.

Jessie nodded. "We just have to find him."

Just then, Erin entered the room from the other side, carrying a tray of freshly baked cookies. She looked excited, as if she were expecting to greet a new visitor. But when she saw that it was just the Aldens, her face fell. She set the cookies on the table by the door.

The children looked at each other.

"Hi, kids," Erin said glumly. "Help yourself to some cookies. I don't think anyone else will be here to eat them."

Jessie wanted to ask Erin again if she was expecting someone today, but something told her not to bring the question up again. Erin had acted so strangely when Grandfather had asked the last time. Instead, she said, "Erin, we're looking for Fergus—have you seen him?"

Erin nodded. "Yes, I just saw him outside. I think he found your book, Jessie. He was carrying it with him. Maybe he thought you kids were playing out in the woods and was coming to return it."

"Let's go before we miss him!" Jessie said, and ran out the front door. The rest of the Aldens followed, though Benny stopped to grab a couple cookies.

"You never know if we might need some extra energy," Benny said with a smile.

The Aldens raced across the meadow behind the castle, the drizzling rain making the grass slippery. Violet tripped and fell forward onto her knees.

Henry stopped and touched her elbow. "Are you okay, Violet?"

She nodded and stood up, brushing off

her jeans. "Just a little muddy. Let's keep going."

Just then they saw Fergus at the edge of the property where the woods began. He disappeared into the trees on the same path the children had taken on their walk that morning.

Jessie tried calling to him, but Fergus was too far away to hear her. The children crossed the meadow and followed him into the woods.

"Erin thought he was coming to return my book," Jessie said, "but then why would he be taking it into the woods?"

"And why does he have it in the first place?" Benny said. "You've been going crazy looking for it. Do you think he had it this whole time?"

"I don't know," Jessie said, "but I need to find out!"

The Aldens entered the woods just in time to see Fergus reach the fork in the path they had come to that morning. Earlier, they had chosen to take the wider path, and that was where they had seen the wolfhound. But

Fergus walked off down the other path, and they followed him.

Because the path was so narrow, the children had to walk single file, one behind the other. Jessie led the way. The path curved around some tall, old trees, and over a small bridge that crossed a brook. Beyond the next stand of trees, they came into a clearing. In the center was a small cottage with a thatched roof, and smoke coming out of the chimney. Fergus went inside and closed the door behind him.

"Didn't Erin tell us on our first day here that Fergus used to live in a cottage in the woods?" Henry asked.

Jessie nodded. "But I think someone else is living here now."

Violet pulled out her camera and snapped a picture of the cottage.

As the children stood back away from the house, wondering what to do, the Irish wolfhound trotted up to greet them.

Violet put out her hand for the dog to sniff it. He gave her fingers a lick and she giggled. "Look how gentle you are," she said to the dog. "I can't believe we were afraid of you!"

Jessie handed some of the treats to Violet and Benny, then brushed her hands off on her pants. The kids fed the treats to the dog and he rolled onto his back so they could pet his belly.

"Are you going to knock?" Henry said.

Jessie nodded. "I think I know who Fergus is coming to see." She walked up to the front door of the cottage and knocked softly.

After a minute the door swung open and a silver-haired old woman looked out.

"Hello," she said.

"Hello, I'm Jessie. And you must be Maeve Rowe McCarron, the famous author!"

The woman looked surprised. "Yes, I am. How did you know that?"

Jessie smiled at her siblings, and the other Aldens understood what she had figured out. The night before, when they had been watching for the banshee through the binoculars, Jessie had said she thought the figure in the meadow looked familiar, but she couldn't say why. Then today when they were looking at the books in the library, Jessie had remembered that her copy of the fairy book had a picture of the author on the dust jacket. And her face was the same as the one Jessie had seen through the binoculars. Maeve Rowe McCarron was the woman they had seen walking at night, and the wolfhound was the one making the wailing sound.

"I *knew* there had to be another explanation," Henry said. "Because banshees are only in stories—they aren't real!"

Benny nodded, looking relieved to finally have an answer. Of course, the Aldens still didn't know why a famous author would be walking around in the woods.

Mrs. McCarron smiled. "Jessie, my friend Fergus brought me your book so I could sign it for you. Won't you please come inside and get warm by the fire?"

CHAPTER 9

The Man in the Picture

The Aldens entered the small cottage and stood beside the stone fireplace as they waited for their eyes to adjust to the dim light. Mrs. McCarron invited them to sit in the chairs and on the sofa, and offered them tea from her flowered porcelain pot.

Fergus sat on the far side of the sofa with his brown hat on his lap. His surprise at seeing the children turned to embarrassment when he saw Jessie looking at the book on the coffee table.

"Welcome," Fergus said, looking sheepish. "I know you probably won't believe this, but I really am glad you are here."

"We weren't trying to sneak up on you," Henry said, "I promise."

Benny nodded. "We tried to call to let you know we were in the meadow, but you couldn't hear us."

"That's all right," Fergus said. "We got off on the wrong foot. I have been keeping a secret all the time you've been staying at the castle, and I am afraid it has made me treat you rudely."

"This used to be your cottage?" Jessie asked. She glanced around. A few cardboard boxes sat in a line along the wall, and a stack of dishes sat next to the hutch. It looked like someone was still in the process of moving in. The walls held framed pictures of a family that included a man who looked like Fergus, but younger.

Fergus nodded. "Yes, I lived here a long time. Raised my daughters here, and after my wife died, kept on living here by myself."

Benny noticed a photograph of an Irish

wolfhound on one end table.

"And is that the same dog we saw outside?" Benny asked. He pointed to the picture.

Fergus smiled. "Yes, that's Tully. She's just like another member of the family to me."

"We have a dog like that too," Violet said softly. "His name is Watch." Violet had noticed that when Fergus talked about Tully, his face softened. She had always believed that caring about animals brought out the best in people.

Fergus continued. "But a month ago I moved up to the castle so Mrs. McCarron could move in."

"Because you always help her make sure she gets her writing done," Jessie said with a smile. "Isn't that right?" She was remembering the inscription inside the book they had found in the library.

"Yes, it is," Fergus said, surprised. "Mrs. McCarron has always been a good friend to my family. I read her books to my daughters when they were small, and we all admire her very much. She has accomplished so much with her writing, but now she has become so famous that people in Dublin won't leave her alone."

"It makes me so happy that readers have enjoyed my books," Mrs. McCarron said as she poured more tea. "But I've had an awful time getting any more of them written. The newspaper printed the address of my flat, and people were coming over all the time ringing my doorbell, and calling me on the phone. Then I tried working in a coffee shop near where I live, and in the public library, but people interrupted me there too. I knew I had to find another place to work."

"And around the same time," Fergus said, "Erin was needing more help at the castle. I knew I could move into a room there, and give Mrs. McCarron some much-needed peace and quiet to write."

"But you couldn't tell Erin about that, could you?" Henry asked. "She wouldn't tell anyone on purpose, of course, but if she let the information slip, her guests might be knocking on the cottage door too!"

"Exactly," Fergus said. "And I couldn't let you stumble upon Mrs. McCarron either.

Which is why I was so grouchy anytime you asked questions or talked about exploring the grounds. I apologize for that."

"That's okay, Fergus," Benny said. "And I apologize for putting my shoes on the table!"

Everyone laughed.

"I didn't make things easy on poor Fergus," Mrs. McCarron said, patting his knee. "A good guest would have stayed home and worked in the evening, but I am a night owl and like to get out for fresh air, even though I was risking being seen."

"You *were* seen—by us!" Jessie said. "Only… we thought you might be a banshee."

"A banshee!" Mrs. McCarron said. At first she laughed, but then she turned serious. As an author of a book on Irish fairy creatures, she knew more about banshees than anyone in the room. "Oh, my. I hope you haven't been worrying your host at the castle with talk of a banshee."

"Because of the bad luck?" Benny asked, thinking again of his shoes.

"Well, it's more than just bad luck," Mrs. McCarron said. "Banshees are just characters in myths that help tell the history of our country. But some people continue to believe in them. They say that banshees foretell a death in the family, particularly the death of someone far away. It can be very upsetting to think about."

Violet put her hand to her mouth. "I just thought of something. Poor Erin—I think she has been worrying about someone, and we've probably made it worse by telling her we thought we saw the banshee."

Henry looked at Violet. "You're right. The man in the photograph in the library."

Fergus nodded. "Probably so. You asked whether that was Erin's father, but he's actually Erin's older brother Declan. They haven't spoken in five years, since a very bad argument they had over how to run the business. They inherited the hotel from their father, and he put Erin in charge because she had a degree in business, while Declan had not finished college. Declan thought that wasn't fair because he was the older child. Anyway, they never could resolve their differences, and he went away angry and never came back."

"How sad," Jessie said. "And Erin has been doing things that made us wonder whether she is expecting anyone. Is there any chance that Declan could be coming to the castle?"

Fergus thought for a moment, then shook his head. "He has been gone for such a long time. I doubt that he would turn up now. But maybe Erin finally realizes how much she misses him."

"And maybe all this banshee talk has poor Erin worried," Mrs. McCarron said. "We should go up to the castle now and explain that the 'banshee' is just Fergus's friend—an old woman who likes to take walks at night!"

"I agree," Fergus said, standing up. "Erin deserves to have the whole story."

So the Aldens, Fergus, and Mrs. McCarron set out back down the path to the castle. Tully trotted alongside them, occasionally darting off into the brush to chase a rabbit or chipmunk.

"Tully knows it's almost suppertime," Fergus laughed. "If I don't feed him some dog food soon, he might make a dinner out of a rabbit!"

The group picked up its pace. As they approached the castle, they saw a car parked at the far end of the lane, near the road where the Aldens had picked the lilacs the day before. It wasn't the Davisons' yellow convertible, and it wasn't Erin's van either.

"Well, now I have seen it all," Fergus said under his breath. "I think that's Declan's car!"

A man with red hair a few shades darker than Erin's got out of the car and started walking up the lane.

"That's definitely him!" Fergus said.

When Declan got closer to the castle, he stopped and put his hands in his pockets. He seemed to be considering something. Then he shook his head and abruptly turned around, stalking back to his car.

"He's not going inside!" Benny said. "He's too scared that Erin won't forgive him!"

Fergus put his hands up to his mouth and shouted, "Declan!" But the wind was blowing in the wrong direction and Declan couldn't hear him.

Violet broke into a run. "Come on! We have to keep him from leaving!"

CHAPTER 10

Forgiveness

The children ran toward Declan's car just as he was opening the driver's side door to get back inside. Tully ran with them, howling.

"Declan!" Violet called. "Wait!"

He paused and stood back up, closing the door. Tully approached Declan and nuzzled his hands with her nose. "Tully!" Declan said, rubbing her ears. "It has been a long time, girl."

"We're the Aldens," Benny said.

Henry explained. "We're staying at the hotel, and we know your sister."

Declan winced. He sighed as if he were thinking hard. "Funny you should mention Erin," he said. "That's who I was coming to see. But now I'm not sure it was such a good idea."

Fergus and Mrs. McCarron caught up with the group. Fergus was a little out of breath. "Declan," he said, panting. "It's so good to see you."

"Fergus!" Declan stepped over to his friend and gave him a long hug. "I wondered if you would still be here."

"Your sister never stopped thinking about you, never stopped hoping you would come back," Fergus said.

"Do you really think so?" Declan asked. "I had a feeling lately that I should try to apologize, but I never could seem to get myself to pick up the phone. Then, this morning, I just got in the car and started driving. But now that I'm here I feel a little silly."

"Don't feel silly," Violet insisted. "Erin will be so glad you are here!"

As if to prove that Violet was right, at that moment Erin came running out the front door of the castle, waving her arms. "Declan!" she yelled.

When she reached her brother, she gave him a big hug. "I can't believe it's really you. I've been so worried."

"Worried? Why?" Declan asked.

"Because these children saw a banshee the other night, and I knew it could mean that something bad was going to happen to you."

"Erin, there's something we need to tell you," Jessie said. "And someone you should meet. This is Maeve Rowe McCarron."

Mrs. McCarron stepped forward and shook Erin's hand. "Very pleased to meet you, dear."

Erin's eyes went wide. "Mrs. McCarron, the author? What in the world are you doing here?"

"Fergus is an old friend. He's been letting me stay in his cottage so that I could work without being disturbed."

"Oh, how wonderful!" Erin said. "We are so lucky to have you. But I promise to keep all this a secret. You will be our most important, most invisible guest!"

"Mrs. McCarron takes walks late at night,"

Benny said. "And Tully wails and howls sometimes."

Jessie put her hand on Erin's arm. "What Benny means is that what we thought was a banshee was really just Mrs. McCarron. There was no banshee, Erin. And no bad luck for Declan."

Erin winced. "I guess I did let myself get carried away believing in that superstition. Well, that is great news for Declan and for me, but maybe bad news for the hotel. I think haunted castles get more reservations!"

Mrs. McCarron smiled. "Well, perhaps it wouldn't hurt to let them go on thinking you have a banshee. Tully does have a convincing wail!"

The group walked up the lane and went inside the castle.

In the front hall, Declan gazed around in wonder. "I don't think those theatrics will be necessary, Erin. The hotel looks more beautiful than ever, and you are doing a wonderful job running it. Much better than I ever could have done. Dad was right to leave the business to you."

"Well," Erin said, "there's always a job here if you want one. I think we would make a pretty great team."

"I will think about it, sis," Declan said.

Grandfather came down the stairs and the children filled him in on all that they had discovered. Then they introduced him to Mrs. McCarron, and Violet scrolled through the pictures she had taken to show him the one of Fergus's cottage.

"You have four kind and very bright grandchildren here," Mrs. McCarron said to Grandfather.

He nodded proudly. "I don't think they've ever met a mystery they couldn't solve."

"I'd say this calls for a celebration dinner," Erin said. "And I have an idea for the perfect food. But I gave the chef the night off, so I'm going to need your help."

Benny furrowed his brow. "More black pudding?" he asked nervously.

Erin shook her head. "No—how about pizza? Irish people love pizza."

"I love pizza too!" Benny said, and everyone laughed.

"I think everyone loves pizza," Declan said. "And we'll help you make it."

The Aldens and Declan went into the kitchen and helped Erin mix up dough and roll it out. Violet spread on the tomato sauce and Benny sprinkled on the cheese, then Declan slid the pizzas into the oven. In the dining room, Mrs. McCarron and Fergus set the table, and then Fergus went upstairs to invite the other guests to join in the celebration.

Once the hot pizzas were sliced and placed in the middle of the table, everyone gathered together.

Erin raised her glass. "Thank you all for being here. First, I want to welcome home my dear brother Declan!"

Everyone cheered. Fergus clapped Declan on the back and shook his hand. Tully barked with excitement.

"And I would like to thank Henry, Jessie, Violet, and Benny. Your investigation brought us back together again, and proved that the only real bad omen in life is letting anger keep you away from the people you love."

"To forgiveness," Declan said, and raised his glass. "And to the Aldens!"

"Here, here," said Fergus, then set down his glass and pulled a large book called *Irish Traditions* from a drawer on the buffet table. "Perhaps Mrs. McCarron can give a blessing before the meal."

With the book resting in her arms Mrs. McCarron called the Aldens over to the head of the table. "I know you children can help me choose just the one," she said. Violet and Jessie stood on one side of her, and Henry and Benny on the other. Jessie scanned the page with her finger and pointed to a blessing she thought captured the spirit of Ireland. Mrs. McCarron grinned and nodded, then took a deep breath and read aloud to all the friends gathered in the dining room.

"May brooks and trees and singing hills join in the chorus too, and every gentle wind that blows send happiness to you."

"And now, let's eat!" Erin said.

Everyone dug into their food and shared stories of the trip. Violet showed her pictures to Mrs. McCarron, and the author told the

children more about the history of the places they had visited.

When the meal was finished, Fergus took a fiddle from a cabinet and Declan brought out a special drum called a bodhrán. Together they played a joyful dance song, and Erin and Mrs. McCarron sang lyrics in Irish.

"I think this is my favorite trip yet!" Benny said when the song ended.

"I liked the gardens best," Violet said.

"I liked the library," said Henry.

"Solving the mystery was my favorite part," Jessie said. "And meeting Tully." She rubbed the wolfhound's ears. "Maybe we can come back next year," she said to Grandfather.

Erin smiled. "The Aldens are welcome at Duncarraig Castle anytime!"

About Ireland

Ireland is one of the British Isles, located off the continent of Europe. It consists of Northern Ireland, a region to the northeast that's part of the United Kingdom, and the Republic of Ireland, the country that occupies most of the island. When the Aldens visit the Republic of Ireland they fly into Dublin, the capital and largest city.

Quick Facts
- Population: 6,378,000 people (entire island)
- Size: 32,595 square miles (entire island)
- Currency: Euro

The first official language of Ireland is Irish, sometimes known as Irish Gaelic. However, English is the most commonly spoken language.

More about Ireland

Irish authors have written some of the most famous stories in the world, including *Dracula* by Bram Stoker, *Gulliver's Travels* by Jonathan Swift, and *Artemis Fowl* by Eoin Colfer.

Ireland is full of ancient places. The town of Ballyshannon has signs of Neolithic settlements that go back to 4000 BCE! Other towns, such as Waterford, were founded by Vikings in the 10th Century.

There are some *very* long place names in Ireland! Can you say *Knockavanniamountain*? What about *Crockballaghnagrooma* or *Muckanaghederdauhaulia?* These names are written as multiple words in the Irish language, but their English versions appear as single long words.

You may have heard the old legend that Saint Patrick drove the snakes out of Ireland. The truth, however, is that snakes aren't native to Ireland—you won't find them in the wild! Some large islands, including New Zealand, Iceland, and Greenland, have colder climates and isolated geography like Ireland that have kept snakes from establishing populations in those places.

Food in Ireland
Potatoes have been an important food to Ireland since the 1500s. One favorite dish, called *champ*, is mashed potatoes with butter, milk, and scallions.

Irish stew, considered the national dish, is usually made with potatoes, carrots, onions, and meat such as lamb or beef.

Wheaten bread is a kind of soda bread made with whole wheat in Ireland.

What about corned beef and cabbage? Even though it's commonly eaten on Saint Patrick's Day in the United States, it's an Irish-American meal.

Saint Patrick's Day
Saint Patrick's Day, March 17, has been observed since the 17th century in Europe. Originally it was a religious feast day to commemorate the patron saint of Ireland.

In the United States, Canada, and other countries, Saint Patrick's Day has become a celebration of Irish heritage and culture.

Saint Patrick's Day is even celebrated on the International Space Station!

In Ireland, the day is observed more quietly than in other places around the world, though larger cities like Dublin hold parades.

THE BOXCAR CHILDREN® Fan Club

Join the Boxcar Fan Club!

Visit **boxcarchildren.com** and receive a free goodie bag when you sign up. You'll receive occasional newsletters and be eligible to win prizes and more! Sign up today!

Don't Forget!

The Boxcar Children audiobooks are also available! Find them at your local bookstore, or visit **oasisaudio.com** for more information.

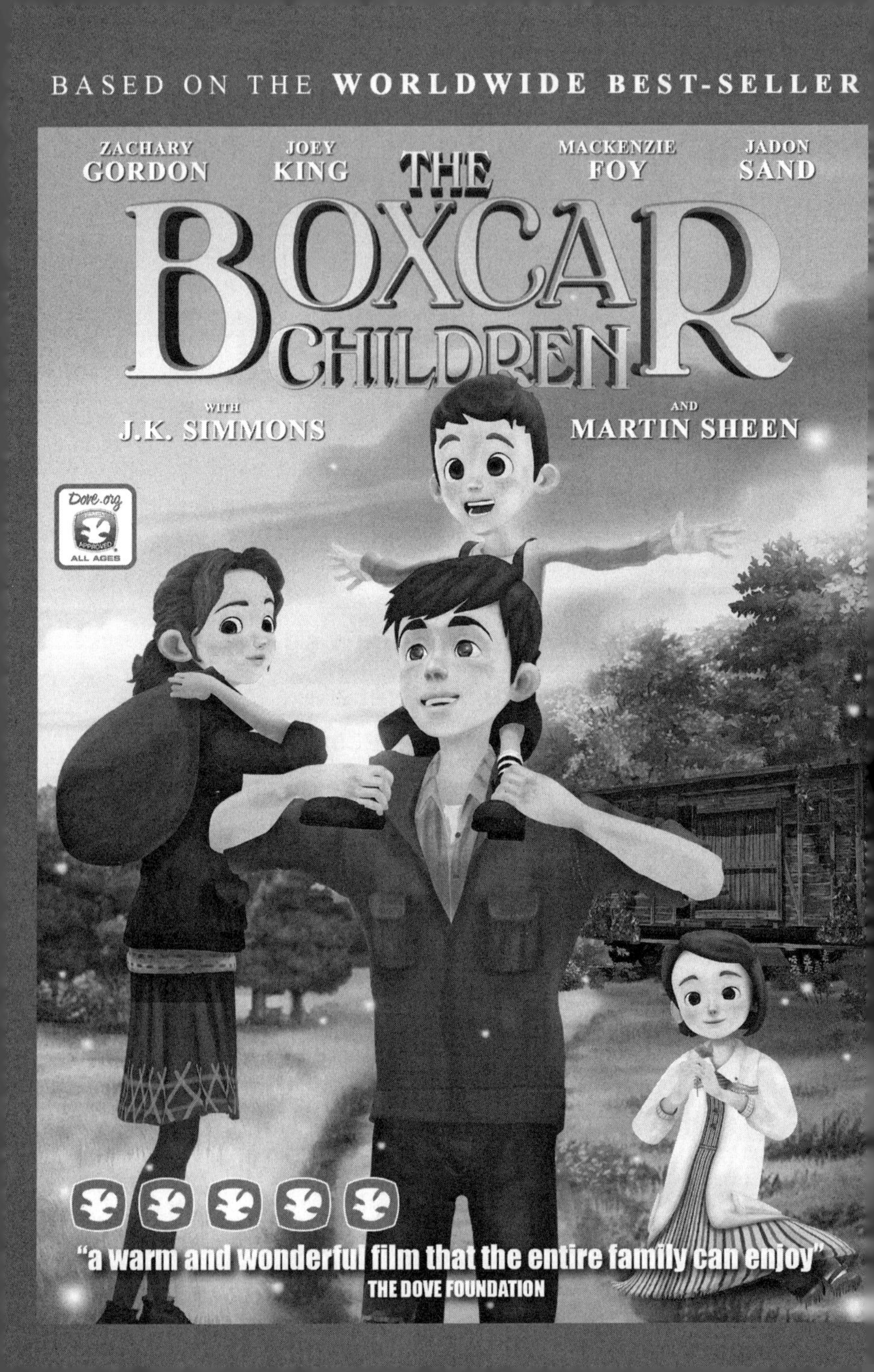

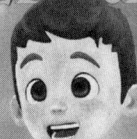

BASED ON THE WORLDWIDE BEST-SELLER
ZACHARY GORDON
JOEY KING
MACKENZIE FOY
JADON SAND
THE BOXCAR CHILDREN
WITH J.K. SIMMONS
AND MARTIN SHEEN
Dove.org ALL AGES
"a warm and wonderful film that the entire family can enjoy"
THE DOVE FOUNDATION

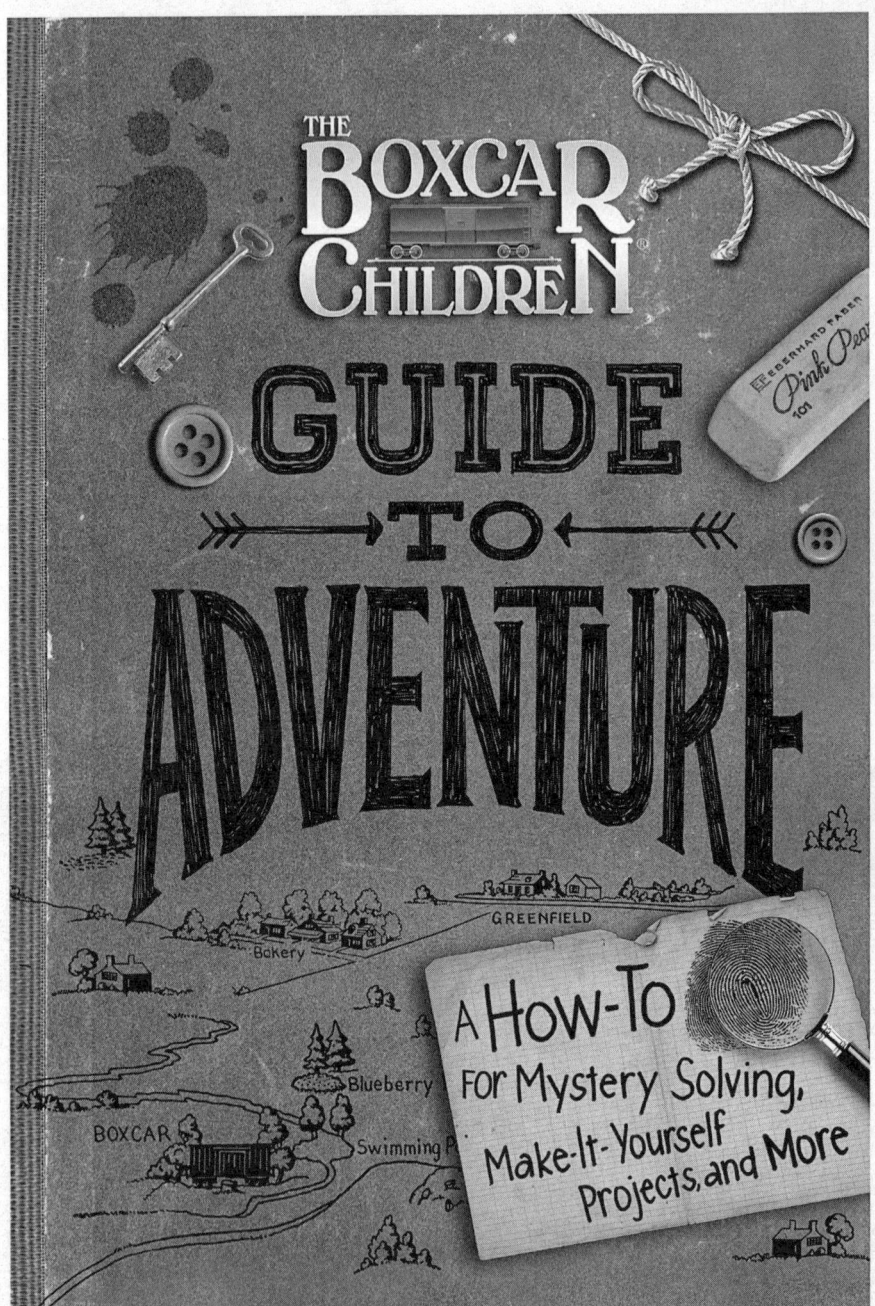

THE BOXCAR CHILDREN®

GUIDE

»—TO—«

ADVENTURE

GREENFIELD

Bakery

Blueberry

BOXCAR

Swimming

A How-To For Mystery Solving, Make-It-Yourself Projects, and More

Create everyday adventures with the
Boxcar Children Guide to Adventure!

A fun compendium filled with tips and tricks from the Boxcar Children—from making invisible ink and secret disguises, creating secret codes, and packing a suitcase to taking the perfect photo and enjoying the great outdoors.

Available wherever books are sold

The adventures continue in the newest mysteries!

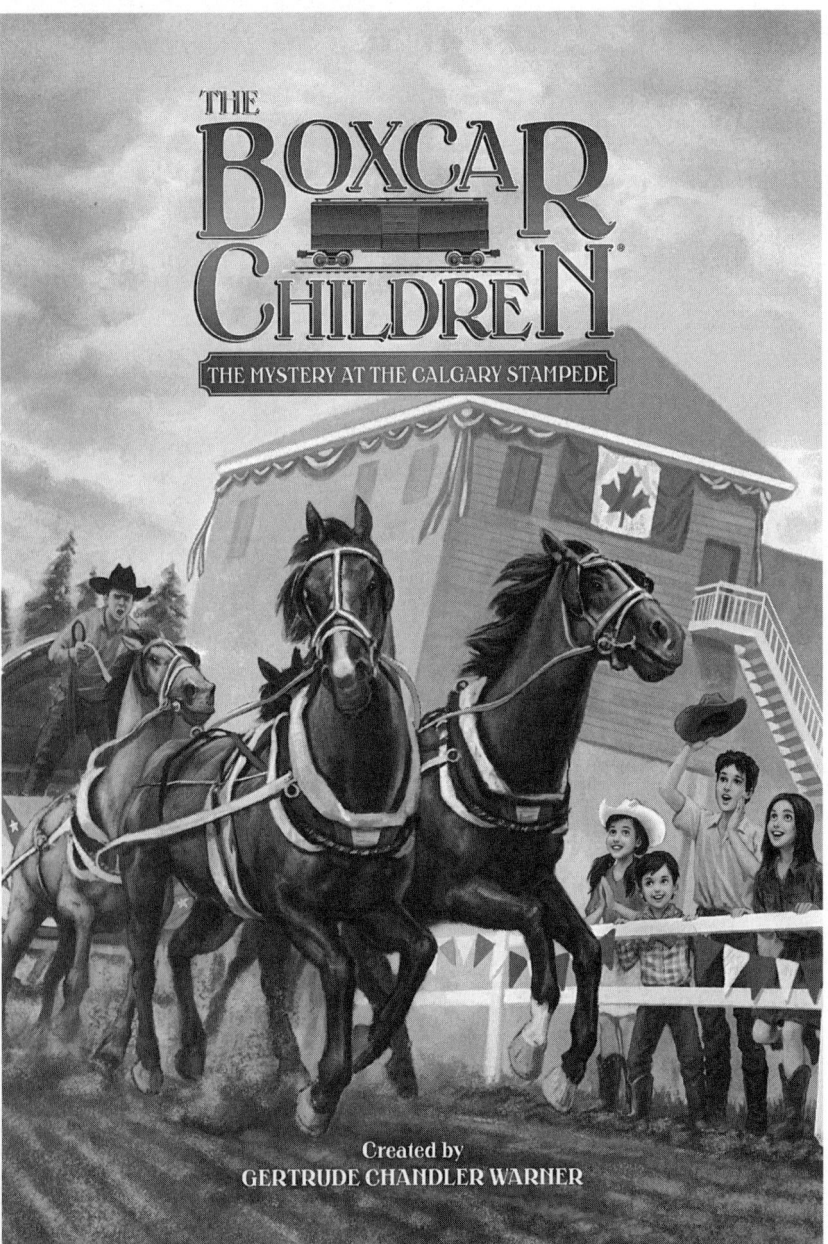

THE BOXCAR CHILDREN

THE SLEEPY HOLLOW MYSTERY

Created by
GERTRUDE CHANDLER WARNER

PB ISBN: 9780807528440, $5.99

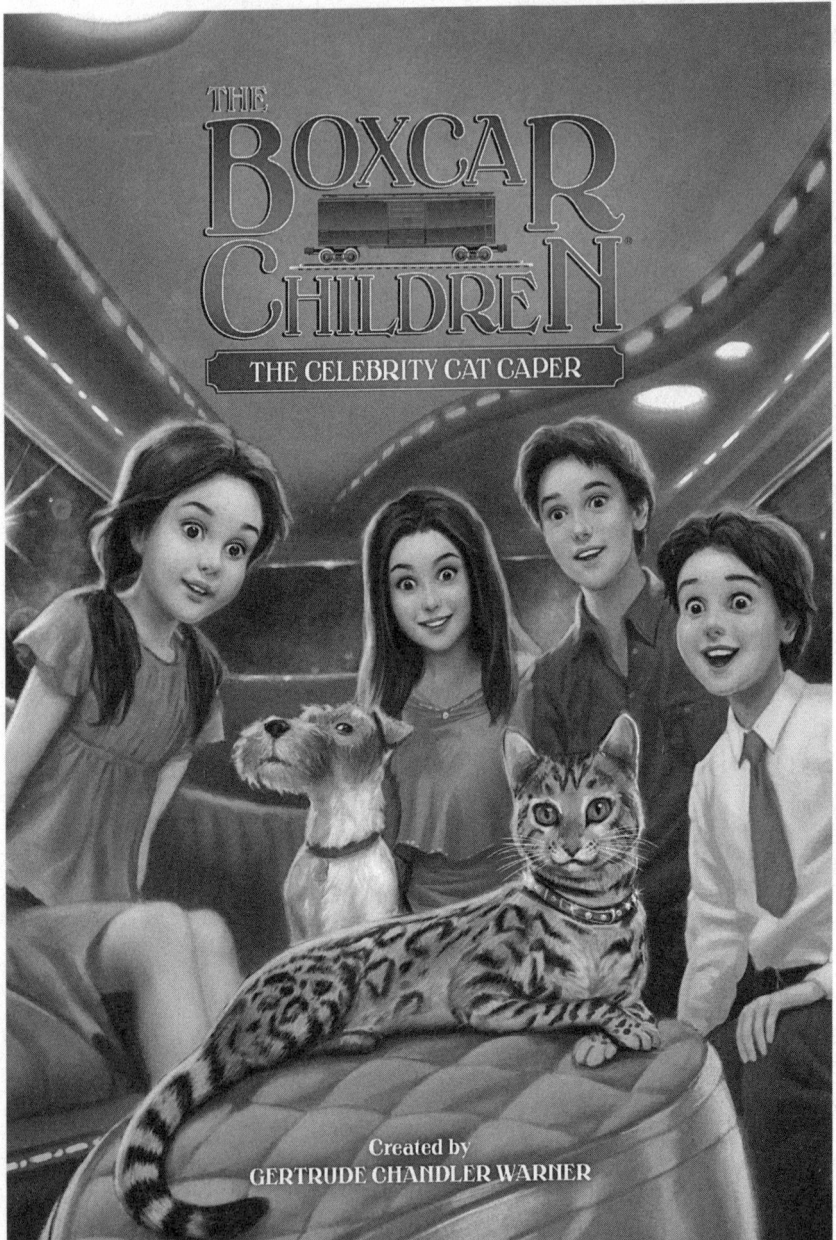

"It's Sunday!" Six-year-old Benny Alden bounded into the boxcar where his brother and two sisters were waiting. A few kernels of popcorn fell out of the large bowl he carried and landed on the floor. "Oops," Benny said. Balancing the bowl in one hand, he bent to clean up the mess, but Watch, the family's wire-haired terrier, got there first. He gobbled up the popcorn, then looked up at Benny.

"No people snacks for you," Benny told Watch. "It's Sunday! Popcorn is the second-best part of Sunday nights."

"What's the *first* best part?" asked Violet, as she took a dog treat out of a container on Jessie's desk and gave it to Watch. Her brown pigtails bounced as she held back a laugh. She was just teasing Benny. She knew watching funny videos was her little brother's favorite part of Sunday night.

The four Alden children were very close. When their parents died, they were on their own, and they found an old boxcar in the woods and made it their home. They had not gone to live with Grandfather Alden because they heard he was mean. But when he finally found them, the children quickly realized they'd been wrong—Grandfather Alden wasn't mean at all. In fact, he was the opposite. Now the children lived with him in Greenfield, and the boxcar was in the backyard for a clubhouse.

Benny handed the big bowl of popcorn to his fourteen-year-old brother, Henry. "Put it near the computer," Benny told Henry. But before Henry set down the bowl, Benny grabbed a big handful. Watch got a few more fallen kernels. "Oops," Benny said again as

Watch lay down at their feet, waiting for anything else that dropped.

Jessie booted up her laptop. At twelve years old, she had a knack for finding interesting and useful information on the Internet. It was Jessie who'd first discovered the Walter the Cat videos and shown the others.

Benny took another handful of popcorn, "I can't wait to find out what the *cog* was up to this week!"

"Cog?" Violet asked. "Did you make up a new word?"

Benny just grinned.

"I get it," said Henry. "*Cat* plus *dog* equals *cog*!" He reached over to ruffle Benny's short dark brown hair. "And Walter is a cat who acts like a dog. That's very clever," he said.

"I know!" Benny said, "But…I didn't make it up." He unzipped his black sweatshirt jacket to reveal a new T-shirt underneath. It was bright blue and had a big picture of Walter, a sleek brown and beige Bengal cat. Under the picture was a single word in gold letters: "COG."

"It's from the mall," Benny said. "I picked

it out and bought it with my birthday gift card." He puffed out his chest so the others could see his gift.

Violet, Jessie, and Henry stared at the shirt.

"Walter is a cog!" Benny laughed. Soon he was laughing so hard he nearly fell backwards into the popcorn bowl. Henry reached out and gently pushed him into a beanbag chair instead. Benny flopped over and continued to laugh, holding his belly. "Cog, cog, cog..."

Henry shook his head. "Come on! Save some laughs for Walter." He dragged the beanbag, with Benny still on it, over to where his brother could see Jessie's computer screen. Violet pulled another beanbag over and made room on it for both Henry and herself.

Jessie typed in the address for the video website, then looked through the posted videos on Walter the Cat's page. "Here's a funny one," she said. "But we've seen it before."

"It doesn't matter," Benny said. "We'll see a new one next. Play it, Jessie! Pleeeaase..."

Jessie clicked on the video so that it filled the screen.

The video began with Walter the Cat

walking across an expensive looking rug in a large living room. He appeared very royal with his smooth coat. On his forehead, between his eyes, was a mark that looked like a *W*.

A woman's voice came from offscreen. "Bang! Bang!" she called.

Walter dropped to the ground and played dead.

The woman commanded, "Roll over." And Walter rolled over and over.

"Up," said the voice, and Walter got up on his back legs and walked like a circus dog.

"Good, Walter," the voice said. Then the video ended.

"That's one of my favorites!" Benny said. "Show another, Jessie. A new one."

But Jessie was scrolling though the list of videos. "I don't understand what's going on here," she said. "We've seen these all before."

"Mrs. Beresford always posts new videos on Sundays," Henry said.

The children remembered the first time they'd seen a Walter the Cat video. One had been featured on their favorite video website. Now they knew the videos were always posted by Walter's owner, Mrs. Beresford, even though she never appeared in them.

"Some of those other cat videos have their owners in them, but she's a mysterious woman," Benny said. "That makes me like her even more!"

"Nothing like a good mystery," Violet agreed with a chuckle.

"Hmmm..." Jessie muttered to herself as she stared at the screen. "Walter's new videos usually make Pick of the Week, but he's not on the list this time. That's odd. There must be a new video in here somewhere."

"Play an old one while you're looking," Benny asked.

Jessie opened another video window in the browser, but kept the window with the video list open. "Here's the latest one. But it's from two weeks ago. There wasn't a new one last weekend, either."

She searched the list while her siblings watched the two-week-old video in the other window.

In this video, Walter panted like a dog and made a barking sound. It must have sounded like a real bark to Watch, who stood up, staring at the screen with his tail wagging.

"Fantastic!" Benny clapped when it was over. "Now play the one where Walter shakes paws."

Jessie loaded the video with a sigh. "Why can't I find anything new?" she muttered.

Henry offered to look over the list. He took Jessie's spot at the computer while Violet and Benny watched the shaking-paws video.

"Strange," Henry said, pushing his brown hair off his face. "Mrs. Beresford has posted a Walter video every Sunday—until last week. She's been doing it for almost a year."

Jessie reached over to the keyboard and typed "Walter the Cog" into a new search window. "I wonder why she stopped and if she's going to start up again."

"Maybe she's on vacation," Violet offered.

"Hey, look!" Jessie said. "I found something."

Violet and Benny came closer to the screen. Jessie had opened up a new browser window to a page called *Cog Chat*. It was a message board where people went to talk about Walter the Cat.

"Now that we know that Walter's nickname is 'Cog', we can find more stuff about him online," Jessie said. "Look at this…"

She pointed at the screen to a message posted by someone called "WalterTruthTeller." Henry read it aloud.

"Walter does not perform his own tricks. The videos are all fake."

"No way!" Benny said.

Jessie found several more online discussions about Walter the Cat. In each one, WalterTruthTeller had posted the same message. "Hold on," she told the others as she tried to find out who was behind that name. After a few minutes she shrugged. "The name is everywhere, accusations all over the place, but I can't uncover who it is."

"Why would anyone say Walter isn't doing his own tricks?" Violet asked. "You can see him in the videos."

Henry read some of the posts over Jessie's shoulder. "WalterTruthTeller says that the videos are manipulated with film software," Henry explained. "Like Hollywood movie making."

Benny moved closer to the screen. "WalterTruthTeller is wrong."

"There are so many strange things going on," Jessie said, as she read over the web pages. "No new videos for two weeks, and now these terrible comments meant to ruin Walter's reputation." She looked at some of the newest messages. "This one says that Walter should go back to the animal shelter where he came from!"

"What do you think it all means?" Violet asked.

"Sounds like the beginning of a mystery," Henry said.

"I think we should investigate," Jessie said. "But where do we begin?"

"I don't know," Henry said. "Anyone have an idea?"

It was silent until the boxcar door opened.

"Benny..." Grandfather stepped inside. "This came for you in the mail today." He handed Benny an envelope. "Remember at the mall when you got the T-shirt, I helped you sign you for the Cog Fan Club. This is the welcome letter."

"Look! It has my address on it!" Benny waved the envelope around. "I got mail!" He opened the letter and handed it to Grandfather. "I can read it, but I want you to. It's faster when you help me. Please?"

Grandfather pushed his reading glasses up on his nose and scanned the text. "Well, now, there's a surprise."

"What?!" Henry and Benny asked at the same time.

"This is a list of fun facts about Walter. Like he's four years old, chases mice, and..." he paused for a dramatic second. "Mrs. Beresford lives here in Greenfield."

"Really?" Violet asked.

"In an old mansion at the edge of town." He rubbed his chin. "I know the house, I just never knew who lived there."

"Walter lives in Greenfield!" Benny said, clasping his hands to his heart. "This is the happiest day in my whole life!"

"And now we know where to begin our investigation," Henry said.

GERTRUDE CHANDLER WARNER discovered when she was teaching that many readers who like an exciting story could find no books that were both easy and fun to read. She decided to try to meet this need, and her first book, *The Boxcar Children*, quickly proved she had succeeded.

Miss Warner drew on her own experiences to write the mystery. As a child she spent hours watching trains go by on the tracks opposite her family home. She often dreamed about what it would be like to set up housekeeping in a caboose or freight car—the situation the Alden children find themselves in.

While the mystery element is central to each of Miss Warner's books, she never thought of them as strictly juvenile mysteries. She liked to stress the Aldens' independence and resourcefulness and their solid New England devotion to using up and making do. The Aldens go about most of their adventures with as little adult supervision as possible—something else that delights young readers.

Miss Warner lived in Putnam, Connecticut, until her death in 1979. During her lifetime, she received hundreds of letters from girls and boys telling her how much they liked her books.

The confound
missing diamond necklace

"The necklace was stolen right under my nose!"

"Mrs. Van Tweedle must have been afraid it might be stolen," said Encyclopedia. "Was that why she asked you to guard it?"

Chief Brown nodded. "She received an unsigned letter last week. It told her to put ten thousand dollars in cash behind the statue of George Washington in the park. If she refused to do this, her necklace would be stolen."

"Wow!" exclaimed Encyclopedia. "Is the necklace really worth ten thousand dollars?"

"More," said his father.

"There is no time to lose. Her room must be searched before she gets back."

"Searched for what?" asked Chief Brown.

"For the necklace," said Encyclopedia. "And the gun."

Read all the books in the Encyclopedia Brown series!

Encyclopedia Brown No. 1
Brown

Boy Detective

By **DONALD J. SOBOL**

illustrated by Leonard Shortall

PUFFIN BOOKS
An Imprint of Penguin Group (USA)

PUFFIN BOOKS

Published by the Penguin Group

Penguin Young Readers Group, 345 Hudson Street, New York, New York 10014, U.S.A.

Penguin Group (Canada), 90 Eglinton Avenue East, Suite 700,
Toronto, Ontario, Canada M4P 2Y3 (a division of Pearson Penguin Canada Inc.)

Penguin Books Ltd, 80 Strand, London WC2R 0RL, England

Penguin Ireland, 25 St Stephen's Green, Dublin 2, Ireland
(a division of Penguin Books Ltd)

Penguin Group (Australia), 250 Camberwell Road, Camberwell, Victoria 3124, Australia
(a division of Pearson Australia Group Pty Ltd)

Penguin Books India Pvt Ltd, 11 Community Centre,
Panchsheel Park, New Delhi - 110 017, India

Penguin Group (NZ), 67 Apollo Drive, Rosedale, North Shore 0745,
Auckland, New Zealand (a division of Pearson New Zealand Ltd.)

Penguin Books (South Africa) (Pty) Ltd, 24 Sturdee Avenue,
Rosebank, Johannesburg 2196, South Africa

Registered Offices: Penguin Books Ltd, 80 Strand, London WC2R 0RL, England

First published in the United States of America by Dutton Children's Books,
a division of Penguin Young Readers Group
Published by Puffin Books, a division of Penguin Young Readers Group, 2007

29 30 28

Copyright © Donald J. Sobol, 1963
All rights reserved

Library of Congress Catalog Card number: 63-9632
ISBN: 0-525-67200-1 (hc)
Puffin Books ISBN 978-0-14-240888-9

Printed in the United States of America

For Ben and Julie Sobol

Contents

The Case of Natty Nat

Mr. and Mrs. Brown had one child. They called him Leroy, and so did his teachers.

Everyone else in Idaville called him Encyclopedia.

An encyclopedia is a book or a set of books giving information, arranged alphabetically, on all branches of knowledge.

Leroy Brown's head was like an encyclopedia. It was filled with facts he had learned from books. He was like a complete library walking around in sneakers.

Old ladies who did crossword puzzles were always stopping him on the street to ask him questions.

Just last Sunday, after church, Mrs. Conway, the butcher's wife, had asked him: "What is a three-letter word for a Swiss river beginning with A?"

"Aar," Encyclopedia answered after a moment.

He always waited a moment. He wanted to be helpful. But he was afraid that people might not like him if he answered their questions too quickly and sounded *too* smart.

His father asked him more questions than anyone else. Mr. Brown was the chief of police of Idaville.

The town had four banks, three movie theaters, and a Little League. It had the usual number of gasoline stations, churches, schools, stores, and comfortable houses on shady streets. It even had a mansion or two, and some dingy sections. And it had the average number of crimes for a community of its size.

Idaville, however, only *looked* like the usual American town. It was, really, most *un*usual.

For nearly a whole year no criminal had escaped arrest and no boy or girl had got away with breaking a single law in Idaville.

This was partly because the town's policemen were clever and brave. But mostly it was because Chief Brown was Encyclopedia's father.

His hardest cases were solved by Encyclopedia during dinner in the Browns' red brick house on Rover Avenue.

Everyone in the state thought that Idaville had about the smartest policemen in the world.

Of course, nobody knew a boy was the mastermind behind the town's police force.

You wouldn't guess it by looking at Encyclopedia. He looked like almost any fifth-grade boy and acted like one, too—except that he never talked about himself.

Mr. Brown never said a word about the advice his son gave him. Who would believe that his best detective was only ten years old?

This is how it began:

One evening at dinner, Mr. Brown said,

"Natty Nat has struck again. He has held up another store—and right here in Idaville."

"What store, Dad?" asked Encyclopedia.

"The Men's Shop, owned by Mr. Dillon and Mr. Jones," answered Mr. Brown. "That makes six stores Natty Nat has held up in the state this month."

"Are you sure the robber was Natty Nat?" asked Encyclopedia.

"Mr. Dillon himself said it was Natty Nat," replied Mr. Brown.

He pulled a notebook from his pocket and put it beside his plate. "I wrote down everything Mr. Dillon told me about the holdup. I'll read it to you."

Encyclopedia closed his eyes. He always closed his eyes when he was getting ready to think hard.

His father began to read what Mr. Dillon, the storekeeper, had told him about the holdup:

I was alone in the store. I did not know any-one had come in. Suddenly a man's voice told me

to raise my hands. I looked up then. I was face to face with the man the newspapers call Natty Nat. He had on a gray coat with a belt in the back, just as the newspapers said. He told me to turn and face the wall. Since he had a gun, I did as he said. When I turned around again, he was gone—with all the money.

Chief Brown finished reading and closed his notebook.

Encyclopedia asked only one question: "Did the newspapers ever print a picture of Natty Nat?"

"No," answered his father. "He never stands still long enough for a picture to be taken. Remember, he's never been caught. But every policeman in the state knows he always wears that gray coat with the belt in the back."

"Nobody even knows his real name," said Encyclopedia, half to himself. "Natty Nat is just what the newspapers call him."

Suddenly he opened his eyes. "Say, the only reason Mr. Dillon thought it was Natty Nat was

because of that gray coat!" he said. "The case is solved!"

"There is nothing to solve," objected Chief Brown. "There is no mystery. Mr. Dillon was robbed. The holdup man was the same one who has been robbing other stores in the state."

"Not quite," said Encyclopedia. "There was no holdup at The Men's Shop."

"What do you mean?" exclaimed Mr. Brown.

"I mean Mr. Dillon wasn't robbed, Dad. He lied from beginning to end," answered Encyclopedia.

"Why should Mr. Dillon lie?" demanded his father.

"I guess he spent the money. He didn't want his partner, Mr. Jones, to know it was missing," said Encyclopedia. "So Mr. Dillon said he was robbed."

"Leroy," said his mother, "please explain what you are saying."

"It's simple, Mom," said Encyclopedia. "Mr. Dillon read all about Natty Nat in the news-

"*Go on, Leroy,*" *said Mr. Brown.*

papers. So he knew Natty Nat always wore a gray coat with a belt in the back when he held up stores."

"Go on, Leroy," said Mr. Brown, leaning forward.

"Mr. Dillon knew it would sound much better if he could blame his holdup on someone people have read about," said Encyclopedia. "He said he knew it was Natty Nat because of the coat he wore—"

"That could be true," Chief Brown said.

"That *couldn't* be true," said Encyclopedia. "Mr. Dillon never saw the back of the man who held him up. He said so himself. Remember?"

Chief Brown frowned. He picked up his notebook again. He read to himself a while.

Then he fairly shouted, "Leroy, I believe you are right!"

Encyclopedia said, "Mr. Dillon only saw the *front* of the holdup man. He had no way of knowing that the man's coat had a belt *in the back!*"

"He stole money from his own store and from his partner too," cried Chief Brown. "And he nearly got away with it!"

He rushed from the dining room.

"Leroy," said Mrs. Brown, "did you get this idea from a television program?"

"No," said Encyclopedia. "I got it from a book I read about a great detective and his methods of observation."

"Well," said his mother proudly, "this proves how important it is to listen carefully and watch closely, to train your memory. Perhaps *you* will be a detective when you grow up."

"Mom," said Encyclopedia, "can I have another piece of pie?"

Mrs. Brown sighed. She had taught English in the Idaville High School before her marriage. "You *may* have another piece of pie," she said.

The Case of the Scattered Cards

At nine o'clock that night Encyclopedia climbed into bed. He lay awake a long time. He thought over what his mother had said to him about being a detective when he grew up.

In the morning he made up his mind.

He would go into the detective business and help people. He wouldn't wait until he grew up. It was summer and school was out. He could begin at once.

Encyclopedia got out of bed and searched through his closet. He dug out a toy printing press, a Christmas gift from his Uncle Ben two years ago.

As soon as Encyclopedia finished breakfast, he printed fifty handbills. When the ink was dry,

he put the handbills in all the mailboxes in the neighborhood.

Then he went home and asked his mother for a big piece of cardboard. She gave him a dress box from the Bon Ton Store, which she had been saving. Encyclopedia borrowed the kitchen shears and cut out a square piece of cardboard. He took a black crayon and carefully lettered a sign.

The handbills and the sign said:

BROWN DETECTIVE AGENCY
13 Rover Avenue
Leroy Brown, President
No case too small
25¢ per day
plus expenses

Encyclopedia nailed the sign on the door of the Browns' garage.

The next morning he sat in the garage, waiting for somebody with a problem to drop in. No-

body dropped in. Only the rain. The roof of the garage had a hole in it.

Rain fell all morning, all afternoon, and all the next day.

Encyclopedia stared at the rain and felt lower than a submarine's bottom. He thought about taking down the sign and going to see what new teeth Charlie Stewart had added to his collection. Or maybe digging for worms with Billy and Jody Turner and fishing off the bridge at Mill Creek.

Suddenly a pair of rubbers and a raincoat appeared in the doorway. Inside them was a small boy.

"My name is Clarence Smith," said the boy. "I need your help."

"No case is too small," said Encyclopedia. "Is it murder?"

"No—" said Clarence, backing away.

"Kidnapping?" asked Encyclopedia. "Blackmail?"

"No—no," said Clarence weakly. "It's a tent."

He placed a quarter on the gasoline can beside Encyclopedia. "The tent is mine. But the Tigers say it's theirs."

"You are having trouble with talking tigers?" Encyclopedia asked.

"Oh, no," replied Clarence. "Tigers—that's the name of a boys' club near the canal. The boys are plenty tough, all of them. But their leader, Bugs Meany, is the toughest one."

"Take me to their leader," commanded Encyclopedia, "and to your tent."

"I'll do both," said Clarence. "Bugs Meany is sitting in the tent this very minute."

After a short walk, the two boys came to the tent. It stood in the woods between the canal and the Pierce Junk Yard.

Six older boys were sitting around a wooden box inside the tent. They were playing cards.

"Which one of you is Bugs Meany?" asked Encyclopedia.

"Me," said the biggest and dirtiest boy. "What's it to you?"

"You are in *my* tent," squeaked Clarence. "I found it. I mended all the holes in it."

"Scram!" growled Bugs.

"You know I found the tent in the junk yard," said Clarence. "You watched me put it up here last week."

"Get going," said Bugs. "I saw you steal it from our clubhouse this morning."

"Mind if I come in out of the rain?" Encyclopedia asked. As he ducked inside the tent, one of his feet hit an extra pack of cards lying beside the wooden box. The cards were scattered over the ground.

"Hey! What's the big idea?" said Bugs.

"The idea is a simple one," said the private detective. "See these cards? They are dry and not the least bit muddy, though I scattered them over the ground. Clarence didn't steal this tent from your clubhouse."

Bugs closed his hands into fists. His chin sprang out like the drawer of a cash register. "Are you calling *me* a liar?"

"Which one of you is Bugs Meany?"

"Of course not," said Encyclopedia. "I'm simply going to tell you what I'll tell the police."

Encyclopedia spoke quietly into the older boy's right ear. Bugs listened. His face grew red, and then redder.

Suddenly he called, "Come on, Tigers! Let's get back to the clubhouse. It's no fun here."

When the Tigers had left, Clarence said to Encyclopedia, "Gosh, what did you say to Bugs?"

Encyclopedia smiled. "I pointed out why you couldn't have stolen the tent from the Tigers' clubhouse."

HOW DID ENCYCLOPEDIA KNOW THIS?

(*Turn to page 79 for the solution to The Case of the Scattered Cards.*)

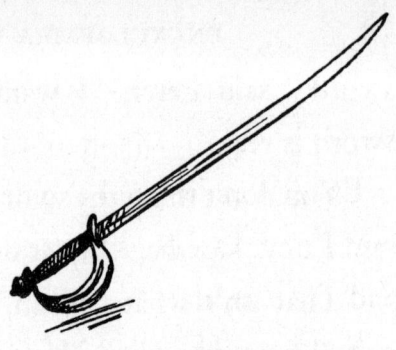

The Case of the Civil War Sword

A boy with red hair stopped in the doorway of the Brown Detective Agency.

"Are you any good at swords?" he asked.

Encyclopedia did not lift his eyes from his book, *How to Build a Nuclear Reactor*.

"What kind of a game is swords?" he asked.

"It isn't a game," said the red-haired boy. "My name is Peter Clinton. I want to hire you."

Peter put two dimes and a nickel on the gasoline can beside Encyclopedia.

The coins clinked. Encyclopedia stopped reading. He looked up, very businesslike.

"How can I help you?" he asked.

"I have a chance to trade my bicycle for a

sword," said Peter. "I want to make sure the sword is real."

"You don't think the sword is really a sword?" said Encyclopedia. "What do you think it is?"

"That isn't what I mean," Peter said. "It's a sword from the Civil War—"

"There are thousands of swords left over from the Civil War," said Encyclopedia.

"I know," said Peter. "But how many belonged to General Jackson?"

"*Stonewall* Jackson?" gasped Encyclopedia. "The great Southern general?"

"This sword is supposed to have belonged to Stonewall Jackson," said Peter. "Bugs Meany says so."

"Bugs?" Encyclopedia straightened up at the name. "You want me to make sure the sword really did belong to Stonewall Jackson?"

"Yes," said Peter. "Then you'll take the case?"

"I'll take it," said Encyclopedia. "If Bugs is behind the trade, you'll need help."

Peter led the private detective to the Tigers' clubhouse, an unused tool shed behind Mr.

"The sword is worth ten bikes like mine."

Sweeny's Auto Body Shop. The Tigers were busy racing garter snakes.

Bugs made a face when he saw Encyclopedia.

"So Mr. Brains is now a Civil War know-it-all," said the Tigers' leader. "Well, well! Maybe you can tell me what Stonewall Jackson did at the Battle of Bull Run."

"Which battle at Bull Run?" asked Encyclopedia. "There were two—one in 1861, the other in 1862."

"Good for you," said Bugs, grinning. "Now don't say this sword isn't the real thing."

Encyclopedia walked to the table on which the sword lay.

Bugs said, "This sword was given to Stonewall Jackson a month after the First Battle of Bull Run."

"If that's true," Peter whispered to Encyclopedia, "the sword is worth ten bikes like mine."

"Twenty," corrected Encyclopedia.

"Read what it says on the blade," said Bugs. Encyclopedia read:

To Thomas J. Jackson, for standing like a stone wall at the First Battle of Bull Run on July 21, 1861. This sword is presented to him by his men on August 21, 1861.

"The sword certainly has seen a lot of use," said Encyclopedia.

"Did you expect it to look new and shiny?" sneered Bugs. "It's more that a hundred years old."

"It doesn't look like it ever was worth five dollars," Encyclopedia said.

"Never mind how it *looks*," said Peter. "Do you think it belonged to General Jackson?"

Before Encyclopedia could answer, Bugs spoke up. "I sure hate to part with the sword," he said. "But Peter wants it so much I just had to say I'd trade it for his bike."

"Trade? You won't trade with Peter," said Encyclopedia. "This sword never belonged to General Stonewall Jackson!"

HOW DID ENCYCLOPEDIA KNOW THAT?

(Turn to page 80 for the solution to The Case of the Civil War Sword.)

The Case of Merko's Grandson

Bugs Meany and his Tigers liked to spend rainy afternoons in their clubhouse. Usually, they sat around thinking up ways of getting even with Encyclopedia Brown.

But today they had met for another purpose—to cheer the boy detective on.

Encyclopedia and Sally Kimball were about to meet in a battle of brains.

The Tigers hated Sally even more than they hated Encyclopedia—and with good reason.

When Sally had moved into the neighborhood two months ago, the Tigers jumped to show off for her. She was very pretty and she was very good at sports.

In fact, she got up a team of fifth-grade girls and challenged the Tigers to a game of softball. The boys thought it was a big joke, till Sally started striking them out. She was the whole team. In the last inning she hit the home run that won for the girls, 1–0.

But the real blow fell on the Tigers the next day.

Bugs was bullying a small boy when Sally happened to ride by on her bicycle.

"Let him go!" she ordered, hopping to the ground.

Bugs snarled. The snarl changed to a gasp as Sally broke his grip on the boy.

Before the other Tigers knew what to do, Sally had knocked their leader down with a quick left to the jaw.

Bugs bounced up, surprised and angry. He pushed Sally. She hit him again, with a right to the jaw. Bugs said *oooh*, and went down again.

For the next thirty seconds Bugs bounced up and down like a beach ball. By the fourth bounce,

he was getting up a lot more slowly than he was going down.

"I'm going to make you sorry," he said. But his voice was weak, and he wore the sick smile of a boy who had taken one ride too many on a roller coaster.

"So?" said Sally. She moved her feet and took careful aim.

"This," she said, aiming another blow, "should take the frosting off you."

Bugs landed on his back, flat as a fifteen-cent sandwich. Not until Sally had ridden away did he dare get up.

Sally was not content to rest on her victories at softball and fighting. She aimed higher.

She set out to prove she was not only stronger than any boy up to twelve years of age in Idaville, but smarter, too!

That meant out-thinking the thinking machine, Encyclopedia Brown.

The great battle of brains took place in the

Tigers' clubhouse. The two champions, seated on orange crates, faced each other. The Tigers crowded behind Encyclopedia. The girls' softball team crowded behind Sally. That left just enough room in the tool shed to think.

Everyone stopped talking when Peter Clinton, the referee, announced the rules.

"Sally has five minutes to tell a mystery. She must give all the clues. Then Encyclopedia will have five minutes to solve the mystery. Ready, you two?"

"Ready," said the girl champion.

"Ready," said Encyclopedia, closing his eyes.

"Go!" called Peter, eyes on his watch.

Sally began to tell the story:

"The Great Merko was the best trapeze artist the world had ever seen. People in every big city were thrilled by the wonderful performer swinging fifty feet above the ground!

"In the year 1922, Merko died at the very height of fame. In Merko's desk was found a

letter. It was a will, written by the circus star. The will directed that the star's money be put in a bank for forty years.

"After forty years, the money was to be taken out and given to Merko's oldest grandson. If no grandson was alive, all the money was to go to Merko's nearest relative, man or woman.

"Forty years passed. A search was begun. At last a man was found in Kansas City who said he was Merko's grandson. His name was Fred Gibson. He went to court to claim his inheritance.

"While the judge was listening to him, a tall woman in the back of the courtroom jumped up. She was very excited.

"The woman said she was the trapeze artist's grandniece. She kept shouting that the Great Merko was not Fred Gibson's grandfather. Therefore, the money was rightfully hers.

"The judge questioned the woman. He had to agree with what she said. She was Merko's grandniece, and the Great Merko was *not* Fred Gibson's grandfather.

The two champions faced each other.

"Now," concluded Sally. "Who got Merko's money—the tall woman or Fred Gibson?"

Sally wore a smile of triumph as she looked at Encyclopedia.

The tool shed was still. The boys looked at their shoes. Had Sally beaten them again? Had Encyclopedia met his master?

Encyclopedia had five short minutes to solve the brain-twister.

Slowly the minutes ticked away. One . . . two . . . three . . . four . . .

Encyclopedia stirred on his orange crate. He opened his eyes. He smiled at Sally.

"You told it very cleverly," he said. "I nearly said the wrong person. But the answer is really quite simple."

Encyclopedia rose to leave. "The Great Merko's money went to Fred Gibson."

WHY DID ENCYCLOPEDIA SAY THAT?

(Turn to page 81 for the solution to The Case of Merko's Grandson.)

The Case of the Bank Robber

"Three dollars and fifty cents!" exclaimed Encyclopedia, as he finished counting the money in the treasury of the Brown Detective Agency. "Business is booming."

"You should put that money in a bank," said Sally Kimball, whom Encyclopedia had made his bodyguard and junior partner. "Money isn't safe in a shoe box."

"Maybe you're right," said Encyclopedia. "Sometimes even shoes aren't safe in a shoe box. It would look awful if a detective agency was robbed!"

The partners talked it over. They decided to take the money downtown to a bank and start a savings account.

It was too far to ride on their bicycles, so they took the bus. They got off near the Corning Na-

tional Bank on Beech Street. As they stepped out of the bus, they heard the sound of shooting.

At first Encyclopedia thought the bus had backfired. A moment later he saw a man in the doorway of the bank.

The man wore a hat. A handkerchief covered the lower part of his face. In one hand he held a yellow paper bag. With the other he waved a gun.

Somebody shouted, "Holdup! Holdup!" Then, all at once, everybody was running, trying to get out of the robber's way.

The man with the gun turned and fled. In his haste he did not seem to look where he was going. He ran into a beggar wearing dark glasses and carrying a white cane and tin cup.

The beggar's cane and cup flew into the street. The robber and the beggar fell to the sidewalk. They rolled about together for a few seconds before the robber broke away and got to his feet.

He raced down the street just as a police car drew up before the bank. Chief Brown and one

of his officers leaped out of the car and ran after the robber.

"We caught him," said Chief Brown at dinner that night. "He led us a merry chase, but we got him. The trouble is we can't charge him with the robbery."

"But why not?" Mrs. Brown demanded.

"Yes, Dad, why not?" Encyclopedia asked. "Wasn't the money he stole in that yellow paper bag he was carrying?"

Chief Brown laid down his fork. "Do you know what we found in that yellow bag of his? Money? No. A loaf of white bread! He resisted police officers, but I don't know how long we can keep him in jail."

"Are you sure you caught the right man, Dad?" Encyclopedia said.

"We'll have a hard time proving it," said Chief Brown. "No one can identify him. And nobody saw the robber's face. He wore a handkerchief over his nose and mouth and his hat was pulled down over his forehead and eyes. This

man we picked up is wearing a brown suit, and the teller at the bank says the robber wore a suit the same color. And, of course, there is the yellow bag. But where's the money?"

"Does the man you picked up have any distinguishing features?" Encyclopedia wanted to know.

"Well, he has a pug nose and a scar running down one cheek. But remember, no one saw the robber's face," said Chief Brown. "I can hold him in jail overnight for resisting a police officer. That's about all."

"I never saw a beggar in Idaville before today," said Encyclopedia thoughtfully.

"Oh, the blind man," said Chief Brown. "He seems like a nice old fellow. He calls himself 'Blind Tom.' I hated to tell him it's against the law to beg here."

"The poor man," said Mrs. Brown. "Won't the Salvation Army help him?"

"Yes," replied Chief Brown. "But he said he likes being on his own. He promised to leave town tomorrow."

"Where is he staying?" asked Encyclopedia.

"At the old Martin Inn," answered Chief Brown. "One of those buildings in the row down by the railroad tracks. Why do you ask? Have you got an idea about this case, Leroy?"

"No," mumbled Encyclopedia.

Mrs. Brown looked hurt. She had come to expect her son to solve a case before dessert.

After dinner, Encyclopedia walked over to Sally's house. "I have to work this evening," he said. "I may need you. Want to come?"

"Oh, boy, do I!" Sally sang out.

The sky was growing dark as the two detectives rode their bicycles down a dingy block west of the railroad station.

"Who lives *here?*" asked Sally as Encyclopedia stopped in front of a run-down hotel.

"Blind Tom, the beggar. He'll be leaving town tomorrow. That's why we have to see him this evening."

"Do you think he can help us?" asked Sally.

"I think so. A blind man sees with his hands," replied Encyclopedia. "Remember how the beg-

gar rolled with the robber on the sidewalk? If he *felt* the robber's face through the handkerchief, he might know him again."

"I get it," said Sally. "If he could feel the man's face again, he might know whether the man your father caught is really the robber!"

"Right," answered Encyclopedia.

"Gosh," said Sally, "I hope he hasn't left town yet!"

Inside the hotel, the desk clerk gave the two young detectives some help. Blind Tom lived alone. His room was Number 214.

Sally and Encyclopedia climbed the dark, creaky stairs to the second floor. They knocked on the door numbered 214. Nobody answered.

"Look, the door's not shut," whispered Sally. "Shall I—"

Encyclopedia nodded.

Sally pushed the door till it swung open so that they could look into the room.

The room was small and shabby. Against the far wall stood an iron bed. A small reading lamp

"Who lives here?" Sally asked.

cast its light upon a copy of the *Idaville Daily News* that lay open on the pillow.

Suddenly the tapping of a cane sounded in the hall. Tap . . . tap . . . tap . . .

Blind Tom came up behind Sally.

"Is someone here?" he asked. "I haven't had a visitor in a long time. I wasn't expecting anyone tonight, but it's nice to have you." He lifted his cane. "Won't you come in?"

"No, thanks!" said Encyclopedia. He pushed Sally down the hall and hurried her down the stairs.

She didn't have a chance to catch her breath until they were outside the hotel.

"Why the big rush?" Sally asked. "I thought you were going to ask Blind Tom if he could recognize the man who robbed the bank this afternoon."

"I don't have to ask him," replied Encyclopedia. "Blind Tom knows the robber, because Blind Tom helped in the robbery!"

HOW DID ENCYCLOPEDIA KNOW THIS?

(*Turn to page 82 for the solution to The Case of the Bank Robber.*)

The Case of the Happy Nephew

The Browns were having left-over meat loaf for dinner one night when the telephone rang.

"It must be important," said Mrs. Brown worriedly. "Otherwise why would anyone call during the dinner hour?"

She hurried to the telephone. In a moment she called to her husband, "It's Officer Carlson, dear."

Chief Brown went to the telephone and spoke with his officer for several minutes. When he returned to the dining room, he wore a frown—and his gun.

"The Princess Bake Shop on Vine Street was robbed less than an hour ago," he said. "I'll have to go out."

"Any clues, Dad?" asked Encyclopedia.

"We have an eyewitness," answered his father. "A man passing the bakery says he saw John Abbot running out the door."

"Hasn't John Abbot been in prison?" asked Mrs. Brown.

"Five years ago," said Chief Brown. "But he's gone straight ever since he came out. The eyewitness only got a quick look at the robber; he might be mistaken."

Chief Brown shrugged. "Still, I suppose I'll have to stop by and question John. I hope he has a good alibi."

"Can I go with you?" cried Encyclopedia.

"*May* I go with you," his mother said. "And drink your milk first."

"*May* I go with you, Dad?" Encyclopedia asked. He gulped his milk.

"Come along if you like," said his father. "But you will have to stay in the car—and be quiet."

"I'll be as quiet as a cat at a dog show," promised Encyclopedia.

He sat quietly beside his father in the police car on the drive to the house where John Abbot lived with his sister and her family.

"Staying in the car won't be so bad," Encyclopedia decided. "The car will be a lot closer to the case than our dining room."

On the west side of town his father stopped the car. "Here's the house."

Encyclopedia saw a small white house in need of paint. An old yellow car stood in the shaded driveway.

"There's John," said Chief Brown.

A tall young man had come out of the house. He was carrying a barefoot boy about a year and a half old.

Chief Brown reminded Encyclopedia to sit quietly in the car. Then he got out and walked toward John Abbot.

"Put the child down, John," Chief Brown called. "And keep your hands where I can see them."

John Abbot started to lower the barefoot baby

onto the sharp stones of the gravel driveway. Then he changed his mind and put the child on the front fender of the yellow car, and raised his hands.

"What's this all about, Chief?" he asked.

"Robbery," replied Chief Brown. "You were seen running out of the Princess Bake Shop on Vine Street an hour ago. The door was broken and all the money in the cash register was stolen."

John Abbot laughed. "I wasn't near Vine Street an hour ago. Why, all day—"

"Look out!" shouted Chief Brown. He leaped for the baby.

The child had climbed onto the hood of the yellow car. He smiled and gurgled happily. Suddenly he stood up and walked close to the edge of the hood. Chief Brown caught him just as he started to fall off the car.

"Thanks, Chief," said John Abbot. "He's my nephew. I'll hold him."

"No, I'll hold him," said Chief Brown. "Just tell me where you were today."

"Look out!" shouted Chief Brown.

"Anyone who says he saw me coming out of the Princess Bake Shop an hour ago is either crazy or a liar," said John Abbot.

"Can you prove you were somewhere else?"

"I was miles away," said John Abbot. "Since eight o'clock this morning I've been driving this car. I drove down from Sundale Shores. I got here just five minutes before you came."

Chief Brown looked at his watch. "You drove six hundred miles in less than twelve hours," he said. "Did you stop around six o'clock and talk to anyone? Somebody we can check your story with?"

"No, not around six o'clock," said John Abbot. "I stopped for gas and a hamburger about four-thirty. Then I drove straight through. I didn't break any speed limit. And I had nothing to do with any bake shop robbery!"

"I'd like to think you are telling the truth," said Chief Brown.

"I am. I've gone straight, believe me," said John Abbot.

"All right," said Chief Brown. "I'll have to question the eyewitness who says he saw you. Maybe it will turn out that he isn't sure."

Chief Brown put the baby in John Abbot's arms and walked back to the police car.

"I heard and saw everything, Dad," said Encyclopedia. "How come you didn't arrest him?"

"Because he says he was driving from Sundale Shores when the robbery took place," answered Chief Brown. "He got here just five minutes before we came. I can't prove he is lying. At least not yet."

He slipped into the seat beside Encyclopedia, and started the car.

"Listen to me, Leroy," he said. "Our eyewitness may have made a mistake. He may have seen a man who only looked like John Abbot. A good police officer doesn't put people in jail without more proof than that."

"I believe the witness," said Encyclopedia. "John Abbot didn't just drive in from Sundale

Shores in that old yellow car. I can prove he
didn't!"

WHAT WAS THE PROOF?

*(Turn to page 84 for the solution to
The Case of the Happy Nephew.)*

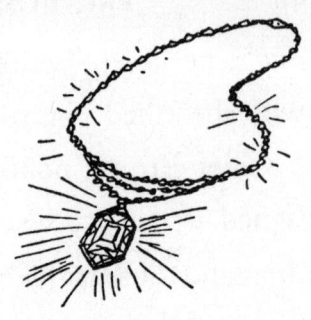

The Case of the Diamond Necklace

"You've hardly touched your soup," said Mrs. Brown. "Something is wrong."

"I'm not hungry," said Chief Brown. He pushed his chair back from the dining table.

"It's that Van Tweedle case," said Mrs. Brown. "Now stop blaming yourself."

"What happened, Dad?" asked Encyclopedia.

"I wish I knew," answered his father. "Last night I was at Mrs. Van Tweedle's yearly party for the Community Chest Drive. I was guarding a diamond necklace."

He drew a deep breath. "The necklace was stolen right under my nose!"

"Mrs. Van Tweedle must have been afraid it

might be stolen," said Encyclopedia. "Was that why she asked you to guard it?"

Chief Brown nodded. "She received an unsigned letter last week. It told her to put ten thousand dollars in cash behind the statue of George Washington in the park. If she refused to do this, her necklace would be stolen."

"Wow!" exclaimed Encyclopedia. "Is the necklace really worth ten thousand dollars?"

"More," said his father. "Want the facts?"

Encyclopedia closed his eyes and prepared for some hard thinking. "Go ahead, Dad."

"Mrs. Van Tweedle planned to give the necklace away during the party," Chief Brown began. "That is, she was going to sell it to the highest bidder on the stroke of midnight. The money was to go to the Community Chest.

"To show off the necklace, Mrs. Van Tweedle's old college roommate, Miss Stark, wore it at the party. At first, I didn't let Miss Stark out of my sight.

"Around eleven o'clock Miss Stark said she

felt ill. She went upstairs to the guest room. She said she wanted to rest a little while.

"I went into the room ahead of her. I wanted to make sure no one was there. Then I had her lock the door. And I stood guard in the hall.

"Ten minutes passed. Suddenly I heard her scream. A few seconds later, two shots rang out. I called to Miss Stark. She didn't answer.

"I broke down the locked door. Miss Stark was lying on the bed in a faint. The necklace was gone from her neck.

"When she came to, she could tell me little. Everything had happened so quickly. She had heard nothing. And she had fainted before she could see the thief, she said.

"The thief must have got in and out by the window. Two bullets were in the wall above the bed. Miss Stark was lucky that she wasn't killed!"

Encyclopedia's father finished speaking. A silence fell over the Browns' dining room.

Then Encyclopedia asked one question:

"Was Miss Stark left alone in the room after you broke in?"

Chief Brown looked surprised at this question. He thought a bit before answering.

"Let me see. . . . I was with her all the time. Mrs. Van Tweedle came up to the room as soon as she heard the racket. Then the doctor came. He took Miss Stark directly to the hospital. He never left her side."

"The hospital?" said Mrs. Brown. "The poor girl. She must have had a terrible scare!"

"She was pretty badly shaken," said Chief Brown. "The doctor ordered complete rest and quiet. She has to stay in the hospital until tomorrow."

"Good," said Encyclopedia, opening his eyes. "But there is no time to lose. Her room must be searched before she gets back."

"Searched for what?" asked Chief Brown.

"For the necklace," said Encyclopedia. "And the gun."

"Leroy!" exclaimed Mrs. Brown. "Do you think the thief would be so silly as to leave the necklace and the gun behind?"

"She did," said Encyclopedia calmly. "She had no choice."

"*She!*" gasped Chief Brown. "Do you mean Miss Stark? What makes you think she did it?"

"It's quite simple," said Encyclopedia. "First she tried to get ten thousand dollars out of her old classmate by writing that letter."

"But the letter didn't work," Chief Brown said. "Mrs. Van Tweedle hired me to guard the necklace. The letter only made it tougher for Miss Stark."

"She didn't think it would," Encyclopedia pointed out. "She must have talked Mrs. Van Tweedle into letting her wear the necklace at the party."

"The whole idea sounds pretty weak to me," said Chief Brown. "Think how fast Miss Stark would have had to work. She would have had to

hide the necklace and the gun after she fired the two shots into the wall. She must have known I'd break down the door the instant I heard the gun go off in the room."

"She hid the necklace before she fired the shots," said Encyclopedia.

"Well, if you are right, the gun and the necklace are still in the room," said Chief Brown. "I'll telephone one of my men to search it right away."

An hour later Officer Murphy called back. Mrs. Van Tweedle's guest room had been searched. The necklace and the gun had been found, hidden in a hatbox on a closet shelf.

The Browns had finished dinner. Encyclopedia was in the kitchen drying dishes for his mother when he heard the news.

"Miss Stark expects to leave the hospital tomorrow a rich woman," said Encyclopedia.

"All she had to do, she thought, was to go back to the room and pick up the hatbox with the gun and necklace," said Chief Brown.

He was drying dishes when he heard the news.

"She might have got away with it," said Encyclopedia. "But every crook makes one mistake!"

WHAT WAS MISS STARK'S MISTAKE?

(Turn to page 85 for the solution to The Case of the Diamond Necklace.)

The Case of the Knife in the Watermelon

Mr. Patch was the first grownup to come to the Brown Detective Agency. He was carrying a watermelon.

Mr. Patch owned a grocery store. He showed the watermelon to Encyclopedia. It had a knife buried in it up to the handle.

"Find the boy who owns this knife!" roared Mr. Patch. "Look what he did!"

Encyclopedia looked at the watermelon. "Stabbing a watermelon isn't against the law," he pointed out. "I mean, it's not the same as stabbing a person."

"The knife *ended* in my watermelon," Mr. Patch shouted. "It *started* in the window of my storeroom."

"Someone used the knife to break into your storeroom?"

"And to open my money box!" cried Mr. Patch.

"How much was stolen?" asked Encyclopedia.

"The thief didn't have time to take anything," said Mr. Patch, in a calmer voice. "He heard me coming and he got scared. When he started to run, he tripped and fell. His knife plunged into this watermelon. He didn't have time to pull it out."

"Did you see his face?"

Mr. Patch shook his head. "No, but I did see he had the letter *L* on the back of his jacket."

"That means he's a Lion—a member of the boys' club on Woodburn Avenue," said Encyclopedia. "A real lead!"

The private detective stepped closer to the watermelon. The knife had plunged into it so deeply that only the carved wood handle showed above the green skin.

Mr. Patch laid a quarter on the gasoline can. "Find the owner of this knife, quick!"

"I'm sorry," replied Encyclopedia, thinking he would have to charge for expenses on this case. "I'll need a little time. I have to buy a fingerprint kit. Then I have to dust the handle of the knife and—"

"There are no fingerprints," said Mr. Patch heavily. "I wiped them off."

"Y-you wiped them off?" said Encyclopedia weakly.

Mr. Patch explained. "My cat knocked a bag of flour off a shelf. It broke and spilled over the watermelon and knife. I wiped off the flour—"

"And the fingerprints too!" Encyclopedia clasped his head and moaned. Then he looked up. "Still, the thief doesn't know that you wiped off his fingerprints—"

Encyclopedia took out his handkerchief. He wrapped it carefully around the handle of the knife.

"That does it," he said. "That makes it *look* as

though we have fingerprints we are trying to save. The thief may try to wipe them off, and give himself away. We'll have to watch all the Lions. Let's go—"

Encyclopedia got into Mr. Patch's truck. They drove over to Woodburn Avenue. Four Lions—John, Frank, Corky, and Buster—were outside the club, working on the engine of an old black car.

Although few in number, the Lions were all big boys—bigger than Bugs Meany. But Mr. Patch was bigger than any of them. He had strong hands and big arms. So the Lions listened when Encyclopedia spoke.

"Do you see this watermelon?" he asked. "Now I take off the handkerchief. There! What do you see?"

"The handle . . ." said Buster.

". . . of a knife," said Corky.

"Very interesting," said John.

"So what?" said Frank.

"There are no fingerprints," said Mr. Patch.

"The knife," said Encyclopedia, "was used in an attempt to rob Mr. Patch's store."

"The knife. . . " said Buster.

". . . doesn't belong . . ." said Corky.

". . . to any . . ." said John.

". . . of us," said Frank.

"Maybe not. But the police will probably take your fingerprints," said Encyclopedia. "If the guilty boy steps forward now, Mr. Patch will ask the police not to be too hard on him."

The Lions looked serious. Mr. Patch looked serious. The only boy detective in the state looked serious.

But that was all.

"It's not working the way you planned," said Mr. Patch in a whisper. "None of them has tried to wipe the handle of the knife."

Encyclopedia nodded. "Leave the knife in the watermelon, just as it is. Don't touch it," he whispered back.

To the Lions he said, "The police will break up your club if they find one of you is a thief."

The Lions stopped looking serious. They looked scared.

Suddenly John said softly, "Frank owns a knife like that."

"A lot of fellows own knives with carved handles," retorted Frank. "Cut it out!"

"You showed me yours yesterday," John shot back. "You even tried to get me to hold it. Why, *my* fingerprints might be on that handle!"

"It's not the same knife," said Frank. "So quit worrying."

"I lost my knife last month," Buster said. "Everyone knows I did. Where is your knife, Corky?"

"I lost mine, too," said Corky. "This one couldn't be my knife, anyway. Mine has a blade a half inch longer."

None of the Lions remembered what the others' knives really looked like. They began to argue loudly. Each boy tried to put himself in the clear.

"Too bad," muttered Mr. Patch. "They are

scared and fighting among themselves. But none of them has touched the knife to try to get rid of the fingerprints. Your plan didn't work."

"Yes, it did," said Encyclopedia. "I know whose knife it is."

HOW DID HE KNOW WHOSE
KNIFE IT WAS?

(Turn to page 86 for the solution to The Case of the Knife in the Watermelon.)

The Case of the Missing Roller Skates

Between nine and nine-thirty on Tuesday morning Sally Kimball's roller skates disappeared from the waiting room in Dr. Vivian Wilson's office.

And where was Encyclopedia Brown, boy detective? He was not ten feet away from the scene of the crime. He was sitting in a chair, with his eyes shut and his mouth wide open!

In a way, he had an excuse.

Dr. Wilson was pulling one of Encyclopedia's teeth.

"There!" said Dr. Wilson. He said it cheerfully, as if he were handing Encyclopedia an ice cream cone instead of a tooth.

"Ugh!" said Encyclopedia.

Dr. Wilson said, "All right. Hop down from the chair."

Encyclopedia hopped down and put the tooth in his pocket. He was going to give it to Charlie Stewart, who collected teeth and kept them in a flowered cookie jar.

Encyclopedia went into the waiting room. The chair on which he had left Sally's roller skates was empty!

He looked behind the chair. He dropped to his knees and looked under the chair.

"The skates—they're gone!" he exclaimed.

"Are you sure you brought them with you?" asked Dr. Wilson.

"I'm sure," answered Encyclopedia. "They were broken. I fixed them last night for my partner, Sally Kimball. I was going to take them over to her house on my way home from your office."

Dr. Wilson shook his head sadly. "I'm afraid you will never get them back."

But Dr. Wilson knew nothing about detective work. Encyclopedia liked the dentist, though he felt that Vivian was a better first name for a woman than a man.

"The skates—they're gone!"

"I'll find the skates," said the boy detective. He spoke with certainty. But he felt no such thing. What he felt was the blow to his pride; it hurt worse than his jaw.

Imagine a detective being robbed!

In the corridor outside Dr. Wilson's office, Encyclopedia leaned against the wall. He closed his eyes and did some deep thinking.

Dr. Wilson's office was on the ground floor of the new Medical Building. The building had three floors and fifteen offices. All the offices were used by doctors or dentists.

What if the thief had followed him into the building in order to steal the skates? Then the case was closed. "I could spend the rest of my life looking through closets, school lockers, and garages all over Idaville," Encyclopedia thought.

But suppose the thief had simply come into the building to see a doctor. Suppose, on his way in, he had noticed a boy carrying a pair of roller skates. Well, that was something else!

Encyclopedia reasoned further. "The thief could be a grownup, a boy, or a girl."

He ruled out a grownup. First, because it was unlikely that a grownup would steal an old pair of small skates. Second, because a grownup would be too hard to catch. Too many men and women went in and out of the Medical Building every hour.

"I'll have to act on the idea that the thief is a boy or girl," he decided. "It's a long chance, but the only one I have."

He opened his eyes. The case called for plain, old-fashioned police leg work!

Encyclopedia began on the ground floor. He asked the same question in every office: "Were any boys or girls here to see the doctor this morning?"

The answer was the same in every office: "No."

Things looked hopeless. But on the top floor he finally got a lead. The nurse in room 301 told

him a boy named Billy Haggerty had been there this morning to have a sprained wrist treated.

Encyclopedia asked in the last two offices, just to be sure. Neither doctor had treated children that morning.

Billy Haggerty became suspect number one!

Encyclopedia got Billy Haggerty's address from the nurse in room 301. He hurried back to Dr. Wilson's office to use the telephone. He called Sally. He told her to meet him in front of the Haggertys' house in half an hour.

"We may have some rough going ahead of us," he warned.

But Billy Haggerty turned out to be only an inch taller than Encyclopedia, and shorter than Sally.

Billy drew himself up to his full height at Encyclopedia's first question:

"Were you in Dr. Vivian Wilson's office this morning?"

"Naw," snapped Billy. "I don't know any Dr. Wilson."

"You didn't ask anyone about Dr. Wilson?" put in Sally.

"I never heard of him before you spoke his name," said Billy.

"Then you went straight to your own doctor on the third floor?" said Encyclopedia.

"Yeah. Dr. Stanton in room 301. What's it to you?"

"Dr. Wilson's office is down the hall from both the stairs and the elevator," said Encyclopedia thoughtfully. "You wouldn't pass his office going up or coming down."

"I don't know where his office is, and I don't care," said Billy. "It's none of your business where I was."

"We just want to be sure you weren't in Dr. Vivian Wilson's office this morning. That's all," said Sally.

"Well, I wasn't. I had a sprained wrist, not a toothache. So why should I go near his office?" demanded Billy. "I don't like snoopers. What are you after?"

"A pair of roller skates," said Encyclopedia. "Do you mind returning them? You've given yourself away."

WHAT GAVE BILLY AWAY?

(Turn to page 87 for the solution to The Case of the Missing Roller Skates.)

The Case of the Champion Egg Spinner

Mr. O'Hara made the biggest and best chocolate ice cream sodas in Idaville. He used a double helping of ice cream in each and every one.

Encyclopedia went to Mr. O'Hara's drugstore on hot afternoons. When the detective business began to pay off, he went there on cool afternoons, too. But he never thought he would one day solve a case sitting at Mr. O'Hara's soda fountain.

People who sat at Mr. O'Hara's counter ordered a soft drink. Or ice cream. Sometimes they ordered both.

Nobody ever brought his *own* food.

But one Sunday a boy about twelve years old

came into the drugstore carrying an egg. He put it on Mr. O'Hara's counter.

Encyclopedia was surprised. He had finished his soda, but he sat and watched the boy with the egg.

He was even more surprised when the boy spun the egg on the counter.

"Still practicing?" Mr. O'Hara asked the boy.

The boy smiled as if he owned the whole world. "Just keeping my touch. I've got a big match tomorrow."

He gave the egg another spin.

"He's good," thought Encyclopedia. "He really knows how to spin an egg to keep it going."

The boy ordered a chocolate soda with a triple helping of ice cream. That cost ten cents extra.

Mr. O'Hara made the soda. He placed it before the boy. He did not see the egg spinning toward the glass till it was too late.

The egg knocked against the glass and spun

away. It dropped out of sight on Mr. O'Hara's side of the counter.

Mr. O'Hara looked down. "That's the end of your egg. I'm sorry."

"Forget it," said the boy with a grand wave of his hand. "I have to use another egg in the spinning match tomorrow anyway."

"I'd better sweep up the mess," said Mr. O'Hara. He walked to the back of the drugstore.

Encyclopedia left twenty-five cents on the counter to pay for his soda. As he went out the door, he saw Mr. O'Hara returning with a broom and a dustpan.

Encyclopedia rode home slowly on his bicycle. He stopped to look at the stuffed mountain lion Mr. Eckstrom, the taxidermist, had just put in the window of his shop. The boy detective was in no hurry. It was Sunday, and the Brown Detective Agency was closed.

As he turned the corner on Rover Avenue, he saw that something was up. Bicycles were parked on the lawn in front of his house. Just about the

whole gang was waiting for him at the garage.

He made out Jody and Billy Turner, Charlie Stewart, Herb Stein, Pinky Plummer, and Sally. They looked as happy as six flat tires.

Sally greeted him.

"The boys need your help," she said.

"With what?"

"With Eddie Phelan," said Charlie Stewart. "His egg beats everything."

"Who is this Eddie Phelan?" asked Encyclopedia. "A human egg beater?"

"Stop being silly," said Sally.

"Eddie is the champion egg spinner," explained Pinky. "He keeps his egg spinning longer than any one else's."

"The boys think he does something secret and unfair to win," said Sally.

"Ah, you fear foul play?" asked Encyclopedia.

"Be serious!" cried Sally. "Eddie won everything at the last match—Pinky's glove, Jody's bat,

Charlie's hockey stick, Billy's magic set, and Herb's jackknife."

"There's another match tomorrow," said Jody. "Eddie is out to win Charlie's tooth collection."

"And I just got two zebra teeth," groaned Charlie. "Mr. Eckstrom gave them to me for delivering Dr. Webster's stuffed sailfish Friday."

"Hmmm," said Encyclopedia. "I never heard of an egg spinning contest before. Who thought it up?"

"Eddie," said the five boys together.

"I might have known," said Encyclopedia.

"The boys have been practicing for days," said Sally. "But Eddie will walk off with Charlie's tooth collection just the same!"

"And everything else," said Billy.

"This case smells rotten," said Encyclopedia. "Where do you get the eggs?"

"At the supermarket," answered Pinky. "All of us go together."

"How do you know the egg Eddie got at the supermarket will be the one he uses tomorrow?"

"Each boy picks an egg," said Pinky. "He marks it with a pencil and gives his egg to another boy. That way we know no one can change an egg before the match."

"Who marked Eddie's egg?" asked Encyclopedia.

"I did," said Charlie. "I made a double X on it."

"Tomorrow you'll have to signal to me," said Encyclopedia, "before you start spinning. If the egg is the one you marked, raise one finger. If it isn't the one, raise two fingers. Got it?"

"Got it," said Charlie.

"Now where and when does the match take place?"

"Behind the school at nine in the morning," said Jody.

"I'll be there," said Encyclopedia, starting into the house.

The boys and Sally felt let down. They had expected Encyclopedia to solve this case right away.

"Oh, stop worrying," Encyclopedia called to them. "I have a pretty good idea why Eddie always wins."

The next morning when Encyclopedia reached the schoolyard, Sally rushed to meet him. She was breathless.

"I thought you wouldn't get here in time!" she said.

"I couldn't find one of my sneakers," the boy detective said, looking around him.

Sure enough! Eddie, the champion, was the boy he had seen in the drugstore.

"The case of the champion egg spinner is cracked," Encyclopedia said mysteriously.

Eddie was smiling as he fingered the flowered cookie jar that held Charlie's collection of teeth.

Against the teeth, Eddie was putting up a football uniform. It was a better prize than fifty-three teeth, Pinky's used science kit, Jody's rubber

boots, Billy's fishing pole, or even Herb's old telescope.

"The match is going to start," Sally told Encyclopedia.

Charlie and Eddie got down on their knees. The spinning field was the smooth marble slab under the statue of Thomas Edison.

Each boy handed the other his egg. Eddie hardly glanced at Charlie's. But Charlie peered at the champion's egg a long time. He turned it over slowly. Then he held up one finger.

Eddie hadn't changed eggs. He was using the one Charlie had marked.

"Ready?" asked Eddie, smiling.

"Do something—fast!" Sally whispered to Encyclopedia.

"Get set—" Eddie called.

"Excuse me," said Encyclopedia. "Is this a contest of skill alone?"

"Huh?" said Eddie. "Why . . . of course."

"Then you won't mind changing eggs," said Encyclopedia. "Let Charlie have your egg, and

Charlie peered at the egg.

you take his. The boy who spins his egg the longest wins the match."

Eddie's smile disappeared as fast as pancakes at Sunday breakfast. His hand closed quickly over his egg.

"Are you saying someone's cheating?" he demanded. "Not that it's any of your business, but Charlie knows this is my egg. It's the same one he marked."

"Of course, it's the same egg," said Encyclopedia. "But with one big difference that nobody can see!"

WHAT WAS THE DIFFERENCE?

(Turn to page 88 for the solution to The Case of the Champion Egg Spinner.)

Solution to *The Case of the Scattered Cards*

Bugs Meany said that Clarence had stolen the tent from the Tigers' clubhouse "this morning." That is, on the second day of the rain. Therefore, the ground under the tent should have been *wet*.

But when Encyclopedia scattered the cards with his foot, he discovered that the ground inside the tent was *dry*. This proved that the tent had been put up *before* the rain, as Clarence claimed—and not during the rain "this morning," as Bugs said.

Solution to *The Case of the Civil War Sword*

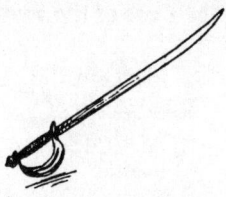

As soon as he had read the words on the blade, Encyclopedia knew the sword was a fake.

The two clues were the words *Bull Run* and *First*.

Jackson's men, being Southerners, would have called the battle by the South's name for it, the Battle of Manassas. Bull Run was the name given to the battle by the North.

Also, the sword was supposed to have been given to Stonewall Jackson in August 1861. No one could have known then that there would be another battle on the same spot the next year, in 1862.

Only after both battles had been fought would anyone have used the word *first* to describe the battle fought in 1861.

Solution to *The Case of Merko's Grandson*

Both the tall woman and Fred Gibson spoke the truth.

Although the Great Merko was not his grandfather, Fred Gibson was the Great Merko's grandson.

The Great Merko, as Encyclopedia realized, was a woman. She was Fred Gibson's *grandmother!*

Solution to *The Case of the Bank Robber*

Blind Tom was not expecting any visitors, he said. He also said that he had not had any visitors "in a long time." Yet the light in his room was on, and a newspaper lay on the pillow.

A blind man does not need a light, and he cannot read a newspaper. So Blind Tom was not blind at all.

Encyclopedia knew then why the beggar had not stepped out of the way of the bank robber. The two men had rolled on the sidewalk together with a purpose—to exchange yellow paper bags!

Blind Tom had slipped the robber the bag holding the loaf of bread, in order to fool the police if they caught him. The robber

had slipped Blind Tom the bag holding the money.

Encyclopedia used a telephone in the store on the corner to call his father. Chief Brown hurried to the hotel. He found the money, still in the yellow paper bag, hidden under the mattress of Blind Tom's bed.

Blind Tom and the man the police were holding in jail confessed they had robbed the bank.

Solution to *The Case of the Happy Nephew*

John Abbot said he had reached his sister's house only "five minutes" before Chief Brown arrived. If John had just driven in from Sundale Shores, the motor and hood of his car would still have been burning hot. Remember, he said he had made only one stop—for a hamburger and gas—during the twelve-hour trip. If that was true, his little nephew, who was barefoot, would have cried out in pain when he stood on the hot hood of the car.

Instead, the baby smiled and gurgled happily. Therefore, the hood was *not* hot.

A cool hood meant that the car had not just been parked after a twelve-hour drive, as John Abbot said.

Solution to *The Case of the Diamond Necklace*

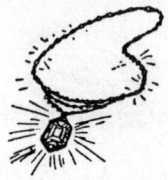

Miss Stark said that she did not see or hear the thief. Yet Chief Brown heard her scream, and "a few seconds later, two shots rang out."

Miss Stark's mistake was screaming *before* the shots were fired.

If she had not seen or heard anyone, she would have had no reason to be frightened. Only *after* the shots had been fired would she have screamed.

Solution to *The Case of the Knife in the Watermelon*

As Mr. Patch said, none of the Lions touched the knife. So the blade was buried in the watermelon all the time the Lions were looking at it.

In other words, none of the Lions could see how long the blade of the knife was.

But Corky said his knife had a blade that was "a half inch longer" than the one in the watermelon. That was his mistake.

He could not have known how long the blade was unless he had seen it before.

The knife belonged to Corky!

Solution to *The Case of the Missing Roller Skates*

Billy Haggerty said that he had never heard of Dr. Vivian Wilson and that he didn't know where his office was. But he knew too much about him.

He knew that Dr. Vivian Wilson was (1) a man, not a woman, and (2) a dentist, not a doctor.

When he was tripped by his fibs, Billy returned the roller skates to Sally.

Solution to *The Case of the Champion Egg Spinner*

Mr. O'Hara had given Encyclopedia the clue to the mystery.

Remember how Eddie's egg had fallen off the counter onto the floor? What had Mr. O'Hara said? Not, "I'd better *clean up* the mess." No, he had said, "I'd better *sweep up* the mess."

He had not fetched a towel or mop; he had fetched a broom and a dustpan.

This told Encyclopedia the egg had broken into *pieces*. He realized that the egg was a hard-boiled one.

And a hard-boiled egg will spin longer than an uncooked egg, every time!

Eddie had to use another (uncooked!) egg against Charlie, and he lost the match. Charlie agreed to give back Eddie's football uniform if he would return the prizes he had won at the earlier matches.

The ex-champion returned the prizes.